HERO ✶ 41

EYE OF THE GARGOYLE

ORCHARD BOOKS
338 Euston Road, London NW1 3BH
Orchard Books Australia
Level 17/207 Kent St, Sydney, NSW 2000

A Paperback Original
First published in Great Britain in 2014

Text © Sam Penant 2014
Cover and inside illustrations by Artful Doodlers, with special thanks to David
and Keiron © Orchard Books 2014

A CIP catalogue record for this book is available from
the British Library.

ISBN 978 1 40832 828 6

1 3 5 7 9 10 8 6 4 2

Printed and bound by CPI Group (UK) Ltd, Croydon, CR0 4YY

Orchard Books is a division of Hachette Children's Books,
an Hachette UK company

www.hachette.co.uk

HERO 41

EYE OF THE GARGOYLE

SAM PENANT

ORCHARD

1

I didn't know it yet, but I was on my way to prison. By bus. My parents had arranged it.

Some parents.

It was a long journey. Felt like days. There'd been other passengers most of the way, but when I woke from my latest doze I found that I was alone. Apart from the driver, that is. I woke this time because the bus had stopped and the driver had spoken. He'd turned in his seat and was looking along the empty bus, at me, all bundled up at the back.

'I said this is as far as I go, son,' he said.

I looked out of the window. There was nothing there. Just old brown land. No buildings, no trees, nothing. I looked out of other windows. Same.

'As far as you go?'

He beckoned, and I slid out of my seat, lugged my suitcase down the aisle. At the front he pointed through his windscreen at an ancient stone beside the road. There were three words cut into the stone.

TWO MILE POINT

'What does that mean?'

'It means that no one born round here, like I was, goes beyond that sign unless they really have to.'

'Why not? The road does.'

'The road's not gonna get any bad luck, is it?'

'Is that what you think will happen to you if you do?'

'I'm not taking any chances. Out you get.'

'How far is it?' I asked.

'Couple of miles, like the sign says. You'll be there in no time. Luck, kid.'

And then I was outside and the doors were closed and the bus was reversing onto the rough ground, and then it was off, and I was alone.

The view wasn't improved by being in it rather than on the other side of a window. It rose and fell and was misty round the edges, and there were all these rocks heaped on top of one another, and there were animals here and there – goats, ponies, a few sheep – standing in small groups like they were chatting about something on last night's telly.

But that was it.

I set off along the road, suitcase banging against my leg, switching hands every now and then to give it a chance to bang the other leg. They might at least have given me a case with wheels on, I thought. I meant my parents, of course. The ones behind all this. The day they told me was still vivid in my mind.

'You're sending me to *boarding* school?' I cried. 'What am I, Harry Potter all of a sudden?'

'If only,' said Dad. 'We could do with a little magic in our lives.'

'Your father's joking,' said Mum. 'This is an opportunity for you, Dax.'

'Opportunity? Being sent away from home is an opportunity? What have I done to deserve it? Is it the window? I told the school governors it was an accident. Even offered to get you to pay for it.'

'It's nothing to do with the window and this isn't a punishment. It's an exciting prospect. You'll be one of Scragmoor Prime's first pupils.'

'Scragmoor Prime? I hate it already, and I don't want to be one of its first pupils. I want to stay where I am. I'm happy there.'

'Happy?' said Dad. 'That's news. All we ever get from you about King's Landing is complaints.'

'Well of course! It's school. Nobody says good things about school. That's no reason to take me out of it and send me... Oh, wait. I get it. You want rid of me. Want me out of the way so you can have a nice quiet Dax-free life. Well, thanks a lot. It's been so good having you two for parents.'

'Don't get upset, darling,' Mum said, reaching for my cheek.

I reared back. 'Don't you darling me, treacherous parent!'

'You should be proud,' said Dad. 'Scragmoor

doesn't accept just anyone. They actually asked for you.'

'Asked for me? Asked for *me*? How do they even know I exist?'

'Ah. Well. Remember last term, having to lick an envelope with your name on it and hand it to your teacher?'

'Sure. I cut my tongue on it. Every kid in the country had to do it – lick an envelope, not cut their tongue. Something to do with supplying a DNA sample for government databanks.'

'It wasn't for databanks, Dax. It was for analysis.'

'Analysis?'

'They say a new gene's been identified – quite a rare one – and the genetic code of every boy and girl your age has been examined to see which among you possesses it.'

'And I do?'

Mum and Dad looked at one another, then beamed at me with shining eyes.

'You do!' said Mum.

I did not beam back. My eyes did not shine. 'What is this gene?'

9

'It's a secret,' said Dad.

'You mean you're not going to tell me?'

'I mean *top* secret. Official. Even we don't know.'

'Oh, wonderful. Terrific. So I've got this rare gene that could make me grow two heads, maybe three, and you're sending me away to give this school with the horrible name a chance to help them *develop*?'

'Exactly!' said Mum.

'Look,' I said. 'Tell you what,' I said. 'I'll behave in class. I'll work harder. I'll even stop answering my teachers back. How's that?'

Dad sighed. 'Dax, you were born misbehaving, slacking and answering back. It's who you are. Can't see you changing now.'

'I can try,' I said desperately.

'Sorry, too late. We've signed the papers agreeing to you continuing your education at Scragmoor.'

'Whoa,' I said. 'Hang on.' There was something suspicious about this. 'Is there something in it for you?'

'Apart from the money, you mean?' said Dad.

Mum glared at him. 'We weren't going to mention that,' she said.

I stared from one to the other of them, and back again.

'They *paid* you? You *sold* me to this school?'

Dad laughed. 'No, no, no. Admittedly, the grant will clear all our debts at a stroke, but we were thinking of you, Dax. You. Your future.'

My future?

Oh boy.

They had no *idea* what was in store for me at Scragmoor Prime.

Who could *ever* have guessed that?

2

As I walked, the mist rolled closer and closer, like it was closing in on me, and the sky got greyer and greyer, like it couldn't wait for night. The two miles felt like ten.

But then the road dipped suddenly, and from the top of the dip I saw that it ended at the grimmest, darkest, most seriously depressing building ever. A high wall surrounded the building, and there were two gateposts set into it, but no gate. My heart did not lift with joy as I approached the gateless gateposts and saw a sign on one of them.

SCRAGMOOR PRIME

I lugged my case onto a cobbled courtyard. Half a dozen cars and a black motorbike were parked on the left of it, under a rusty corrugated roof. On the other side, the right-hand side, there was a long low shed that later turned out to be where horses used to live.

The main building, bang ahead of me, was so old and ragged that it looked like its biggest ambition was to fall down. There were little windows with vertical bars on every level. My gaze travelled up, window by window, all the way to the top of the building. On the roof an ancient stone creature – a crouching gargoyle – glared down at me like it didn't like what it saw. There was something about that look that sent shivers down my spine.

I hurried across the courtyard.

I'd just started up the steps to the front door when a window opened a little way along and a girl with red hair leaned out.

'*Another* one?' she said.

I paused, mid-step. 'Another what?'

'Student. I thought they'd all arrived.'

With that she ducked back inside and slammed the window.

The door at the top of the steps was old and black and covered in iron studs. There was also a big iron knocker. I gripped the knocker.

BANG! BANG! BANG!

I let go of the knocker, and waited.

Nothing happened.

I gripped it again.

BANG! BANG! BANG!

I waited again.

Nothing happened a second time.

I reached for the knocker once more, but as I did so the door jumped back to reveal a very tall thin man with little round glasses on the end of his nose and hair like a bale of hay caught in a high wind.

'Yes?'

'Dax Daley,' I said.

'What?' he said.

'Dax Daley. My name. I've been told to report here.'

'Oh? Why?'

'Well, this is the school, isn't it?'

'It is, yes.'

'Right. I'm one of the students. Or will be once I unpack.'

'I don't think you are,' he said.

'Don't think I'm what?'

'One of the students. We have a forty-student intake and all forty have checked in.'

'You must have miscounted,' I said.

He frowned. 'Miscounted?'

'Students. If forty are expected you've overcounted by one.'

'We're a school,' he said. 'Counting is one of those little things we do. The fortunate forty are having their welcome dinner as we speak. I was grabbing a snack myself before I was so rowdily interrupted.'

'Yeah, but...'

I rummaged in my pockets for the bit of paper

that told me where to come, and handed it over. The tall man peered at it like it had been dipped in something he was allergic to. Then he thrust it back at me.

'Clearly an error,' he said. 'There's no provision for a forty-first student.'

'So where does that leave me?' I asked.

'It leaves you right there on the step. Which I suggest you get off in order to go back where you came from.'

He started to close the door, but I jammed my foot in the gap. Bad move, because it didn't stop him trying to close it.

'Ow, that hurts!' I yelled.

'It will hurt less if you keep your feet out there where they belong,' he said. But he eased back on the door.

'Now let's get this straight,' I said, hopping about on the foot he hadn't squashed. 'You're saying that I can't come in, can't go to this school, and that I've got to limp back across the moor, where I'll probably get lost, and never be seen again?'

'A fair summation,' he said. 'It'll be dark soon

and the fog's coming in. We get terrible fogs here. I'm told that a number of folk have gone missing over the years on Scrag Moor. We had proof of that just last week actually. A man was found down a crevasse, neck broken from the fall, no ID, could have been anyone.'

'Thanks for sharing that,' I said, turning to go.

'Wait!'

I turned back. 'What?'

'I can't watch you walk away.'

'So close your eyes,' I said.

'You'd better come in. You'll have to stay the night.'

I eyed him suspiciously. 'Why the change of heart?'

One of his lofty shoulders shrugged. 'I'm not a monster.'

'If you say so. So you'll give me a bed for the night?'

'A bed? We only have forty. A bit of floor maybe. Have you eaten?'

'Not lately. Scoffed my last energy bar two hours ago.'

'Well, I'll see if I can ferret out a crust in the kitchen.'

'Ooh, a floor *and* a crust. Really fallen on my feet here, haven't I?'

He stepped back, widening the door gap.

'What are you anyway?' I asked as I lugged my case over the unwelcome mat. 'The butler? Janitor? A stand-up who's forgotten his jokes?'

'I'm Withering.'

'Withering? Why, what's wrong with you?'

'*Doctor* Withering, head of Scragmoor Prime.'

'Oh. Right. Thrilled to meet you, Doc.'

'*Doctor,*' he said firmly.

He slammed the door, bolted it, and I looked around at the gloomiest interior I ever saw off a screen. The lights were so dim they might have been candles in disguise.

I took my phone out. 'I better call my folks. Tell 'em I'm not stopping.'

He shook his head. 'Sorry, that won't be possible. No signal.'

'No signal? No phone signal anywhere in the building?'

'No coverage for twenty miles around, and just one specially installed hot spot – in there.' He

18

pointed to a door on the left as you came in. 'We call it the Com Centre, but its use is restricted to Saturdays. That one day of the week aside, no calls, texts, tweets or anything else of the ilk are permitted. We also don't allow the use of communication devices *within* Scragmoor.'

'But that's crazy.'

'It's the way things are here.'

'You're not keen on your students talking to one another, is that it?'

'They have voices for that. Old-fashioned, I know, but there you go.'

I pocketed my phone. 'OK. But as I'm not going to be one of the lucky forty I have to call my parents. So take me to a landline. You must have one of those.'

'We do,' he said, 'and you may use it just before I shut the door on you in the morning, never to meet again.'

'Well, that's the day's highlight taken care of,' I said. I looked around me. 'I was told this was a *new* school.'

'It's very new. Tomorrow is Day One. It's just the

building that's old.'

'Old? It's prehistoric. It looks like an ancient prison.'

'Which is exactly what it was, originally.'

'A prison? You're kidding me.'

'Not at all. Convicted felons and miscreants were sent to Scragmoor Jail for almost two hundred years.'

'Some sentence,' I said.

'Many were confined for life, others stayed merely for days before...' He stopped. Smiled a wonky yellow smile. 'Let's just say that on certain nights, so it's said, screams can still be heard echoing through the cells.'

'There are still cells here?'

'Oh yes. And just as well too. The students have to sleep somewhere.'

'They *sleep* in the cells?'

'We call them bedcells. Sounds cosier. Now let's see if we can locate that crust.'

He spun on a heel and walked off. I went after him.

The first door we passed had 'Matron' on it. The next had 'Dr Withering'. Then there was a dark stairwell with a rope across it and an UNSAFE ENTRY FORBIDDEN sign.

We'd just passed the stairwell when the building exploded.

It didn't really explode, but it was that kind of shock, like a big all-controlling switch had been pulled, because all of a sudden the lights grew as bright as the most brilliant sunshine and every alarm for miles went off at once. I screwed up my dazzled eyes, clapped my hands over my earholes,

sagged against the wall, and, through my slitted lids, saw Withering's mouth flapping.

I uncovered my ears. 'What?' I shouted.

'Power surge!' he shouted back. But he was laughing. 'They were right! Bring 'em together and... ha-ha-ha-ha! Kitchen's down there! I'll be back!'

And he charged off, into the deafening sound, the blinding light.

I stayed where I was, cowering against the wall, till the alarms stopped just as suddenly as they'd started and the lights dimmed. With the bulbs back to candle-dull and the building as silent as a tomb once more I went on to the kitchen, where I found something to eat. Not just a crust. There was much more than a crust. I fed my face like I hadn't eaten for months.

Comfort food.

I jerked awake. Blinked around. Moon at a high window with bars. But in my head I'd fallen, down, down, down, landed with a thump. I was scared, unable to get back up to the surface or call for help. I sat up, but all this stayed with me. I'd been dreaming, obviously, but I still felt like I was underground and couldn't climb up or cry out.

I was on a mattress on the floor of the cell Withering had brought me to after cutting the alarms and lights and returning to the kitchen. We'd passed no one on the way here, seen no one, though every now and then I heard a voice in the distance. Most of the walls were rough stone, undecorated. No nice bright pictures or posters like you get in normal schools. Most of the doors were black or brown, very heavy, with big keyholes, looked like they'd been there for a century or more. This *used* to be a prison? From the look and feel and sound of it, it could still be one.

'You've got work on your hands if you want this joint to look like a modern school,' I said to the Doc as we walked, my suitcase still crashing against my legs.

'Some refurbishment is planned,' he informed me loftily.

'Does the plan include bulldozers and wrecking balls?'

'Plus a fair amount of rebuilding over time. We'll endeavour to maintain the original spirit of the place, though.'

'That shouldn't be hard.'

'Oh, this is nothing. Scragmoor operated as a museum of prison life for many years after the jail closed and most of the subterranean displays have been left intact. I wouldn't want to go down there on my own at night. Spooky isn't the word for it, ha-ha-ha-ha.'

The man was obviously a nutter.

The boys' cells – 'bedcells' – were on the first floor. There were ten of them, five facing five more across an uncarpeted passageway. Like the doors we'd passed on the way, the ones on the cells looked like the originals, with a little panel in each. I peered through one of the panels, into a cell about five metres by four, with a high barred window. The walls had been painted recently – you could smell the paint – and there was a carpet, a new chest of drawers, a wardrobe, a bookcase, a little table, bunk beds.

'No TV?' I asked.

'Not in the bedcells or any other part of the building the students have access to,' the Doc said.

'You mean they can't watch TV *or* call anybody?'

'There's a television lounge, but the satellite dish has yet to be fitted, and when it is, viewing will be strictly limited and controlled.'

'That's censorship,' I said.

'It is indeed. Ah, Mr Banner, did you manage to find a corner for our extra guest?'

A miserable-looking cove in a long brown coat had just come out of the last cell on the right. 'Number 10,' he said, jerking a thumb over his shoulder and stomping away.

Dr Withering motioned me forward. I looked into the cell. It was just like the other one except as well as bunk beds there was a mattress on the floor.

'Which is mine?' I asked.

'With a duvet and a pillow,' he said, 'that's the height of luxury compared to the privations the prisoners of old had to endure.'

'Oh, hang on,' I said, 'I'll just count my lucky stars. Where do the teachers sleep? Not cells, I bet.'

'The resident staff lodge in the former Debtors' Prison in the East Wing. Their rooms are a little larger than these, but they're still cells.'

'Will there be someone to drive me away from here at high speed in the morning?' I asked.

'Drive you away?'

'In a car, to a station. I'm guessing there *is* one somewhere this side of the end of the world?'

'I'll see if there's someone available at the time. The bathroom's the other side of that gate there. Sleep tight, don't let the bugs bite, ha-ha-ha-ha.'

When he'd gone I went into the cell and looked for something fascinating to take my mind off being there. It took five seconds to run out of options.

So I just sat on the lower bunk and waited for time to pass. While waiting I wondered how come I'd been sent here if they'd already got their forty students, and came to the conclusion that they must have realised I didn't have that special gene after all but forgot to update my folks. Still, even though I was still ordinary old Dax Daley, with a long, boring return journey ahead of me, I was *very* glad I wasn't stopping in this dismal, gloomy, spooky old dump.

After a while I heard footstep and voices. I didn't want to be there when the boys I was sharing with came in, so I jumped up, darted out of the cell, through the gate at the end, into the bathroom – which turned out to be the most civilised room I'd seen so far. I locked myself into a cubicle and right away heard some boys come in. They talked in low voices, so I couldn't catch much. A couple of them laughed, but quietly, like they were scared of being overheard.

When they'd gone I waited a minute before going back. Four or five boys were hanging round the passageway between the cells. I slipped by without meeting any eyes. In Cell 10 I found one

27

of my overnight roomies unpacking his bag and hanging things in the wardrobe, while the other, who was much shorter, stood on tiptoe trying to see out of the high window. The short boy glanced over his shoulder as I went in, then turned away again, but the one at the wardrobe said 'Hi' and asked if the mattress on the floor was mine.

'Yeh. Just for the night.'

'What, they run out of bunks?'

'Something like.'

'I'm Marcus,' he said. 'Marcus Preedy.'

I nodded but didn't give my name.

'I can't wait for tomorrow,' Marcus Preedy said.

'Why, what happens tomorrow?'

'Weren't you at dinner?'

'No, missed it.'

'They're going to tell us why we're here, why there's just twenty boys and twenty girls, what the deal is.'

'It's something about a special gene,' I said.

'Yes, but what, that's what nobody knows yet.'

'You're sure it's something good, are you?'

He grinned like an idiot. 'Oh, yes! They told us that much if nothing else. It's something very unusual, they said.'

The other boy, the silent one, went to the lower bunk, pulled a book out from under it and turned his back on us. He seemed even less keen on talking than I was. Facing the wall, his book was in shadow, but he had a little torch and read by its light, like a secret comic in the night.

Marcus Preedy leaned towards me and whispered, 'He hasn't said a word since he got here.'

'Maybe he didn't expect a prison cell,' I whispered back.

He grinned again. 'Yeah. Isn't this the *coolest*?'

He carried on talking about how cool it was to be here, what it might be that had singled out this particular forty from the crowd, and so on, and I nodded and gurned and whatevered without letting on that I wasn't going to be joining him, and finally, at half nine, a voice came out of the wall and told us the lights would go off in fifteen minutes.

I opened my suitcase thinking I would change into my pyjamas, but pyjamas in a prison cell didn't feel right somehow, so I left them and got under my duvet fully dressed apart from my coat and shoes. Marcus climbed the ladder to the top bunk and snuggled down all bright eyed and excited, but the boy on the lower bunk – who like me hadn't changed into his jimjams – didn't move or make a sound. I got under my duvet on the floor and waited for darkness. It came with a clunk, and was total. Right after that the boy on the bottom bunk turned his torch off.

I must have fallen asleep pretty soon because I remember nothing after the lights went out until I woke from the dream I mentioned, of falling and feeling desperate and unable to call for help. I propped myself on an elbow trying to shake the dream and saw – thanks to the moonlight squeezing between the window bars – that the bottom bunk was empty. I wondered where the silent kid had gone, then decided I didn't care.

I lay back down and waited for the after-dream misery to ease off. But it didn't, it got worse, washing through me in great waves until I was so unhappy that I felt like bursting into tears. At home after a dream that I can't shake I go down to the kitchen, find something to eat, watch something prerecorded on TV, but I couldn't do any of that here. I didn't fancy wandering around a building like this in the middle of the night either, but I needed to do something to empty my mind of all that misery and fear, so I got up and put my shoes on.

The moonlight stopped at the door, like it wasn't allowed any further. There were lights in the corridor, but they were so dim that they threw out just enough brilliance for me to grope my way through the gate that led to the bathroom. I didn't need the bathroom but maybe a palm or two of tap water would rinse the dream out of my head.

The misery grew and grew the further I got from the cell, and as I reached the bathroom something tugged at me – mentally, not physically – and I didn't seem to have much choice but to go where the tug took me, so I went, until I stood before a sign that I could just make out in the last of the light.

IT IS DANGEROUS TO GO BEYOND THIS POINT

If there was anything beyond the sign I couldn't see it, thanks to the deep, deep darkness. I stared into the black nothingness. I didn't want to go any further, I really didn't, but I was still being tugged by something I couldn't resist, and still filled with that stonking misery, so I walked round the sign.

Walked round it, and took one step, then another, and another, step after cautious step, on and on, into the ever deeper dark, until—

'What are you doing out here?'

I stopped, skin prickling all over.

'Who's that?' I whispered.

And then I saw eyes. Bright green ones. Nothing else, just two bright green eyes. And then the voice came again.

'Oh, it's you. Why are you wandering round in the dark?'

4

'You can *see* me?' I said to the bright green eyes.

'Of course I can see you. How else would I know you're there?'

'But...how?'

'I'm Cat,' the voice said.

'A *cat*?'

'Cat. It's a nickname. Started out as Cats' Eyes, because my eyes glow in the dark.'

'But it's so...'

'Dark? Not for me. Want me to prove it?'

'Prove it? How could you pr— ow!'

Something had twisted my nose.

'Convinced?' the girl said.

'You didn't have to do that,' I said, holding my nose.

'Believe me now, though, do you?'

'That you can see in total darkness? No, of course I— ow!'

She'd tugged my left ear.

I jumped back, out of reach.

'Oh, think you can get away, do you?' she said.

'Agh!'

She'd stamped on one of my feet.

'Get off me,' I said. 'I was miserable enough already, without this.'

'Miserable? Why? Missing Mummy?'

'No, I had a bad dream that's staying with me.'

'Aww, diddums.'

'You said, "Oh, it's you" just now. Have we met?'

'Yes. When you arrived. I opened a window.'

'Oh, *you*,' I said. 'Why are you wandering round in the dark?'

'That was my question.'

'Yes, and now it's mine.'

'I heard a crash somewhere along here. What's your excuse?'

'I don't need one. I'm going back n— oh!'

'I didn't touch you,' she said.

'No, it's this...wooh!'

'What?'

'Unhappiness. Fear.'

'Don't worry,' she said. 'I'll guide you.'

'It's not me. I thought it was the dream, but...' I nodded into the darkness. 'It feels like it's coming from down there somewhere.'

'That's one of the most ruined parts of the building. It's not safe there.'

'Well that's where I'm getting it from. But it's just a feeling.'

'Feelings like that should be investigated. Specially here, now.'

'What do you mean, now?'

'With you here. Us.'

She must have turned away because suddenly I couldn't see her eyes. Then I heard the scuff of her feet moving away.

'Where are you going?' I called.

'To investigate.'

'But if it's not safe...'

'It goes off in different directions here,' she said from the distance. 'Loads more cells, really awful ones, not used for an age. Are you still getting that feeling?'

'Yes. From further on, past your voice.'

'Which way?'

'How can I say when I can't see a thing?'

'Point.'

I pointed into the deep, deep dark.

'The way turns just there,' Cat said. 'You won't be able to guide me once I go round the corner. You better come too.'

'Oh, I don't know about that,' I said.

'There's nothing to worry about, I'll be with you.'

Her eyes were coming back. I knew they were her eyes, I knew they were in a human skull, but it still creeped me out seeing them floating towards me in the total blackness. The creeped-outness hit the ceiling when an invisible hand gripped my arm.

'Stop wriggling,' she said. 'Just go where I lead you and lift your feet so you don't trip over any rubble or anything.'

When we set off – faster than I liked – I shut my eyes, even though it made no difference. The floor was very uneven, and I stumbled now and then, but Cat kept her grip on my arm and I stayed more or less upright.

'The feeling's getting stronger,' I said after a minute. 'Anything here?'

'Just more cells.'

'Wait!'

I stopped suddenly, forcing her to stop with me.

'What?' she asked.

'See where I'm pointing? It's coming from there.'

'Catch hold of this while I take a look,' she said, curling my hand round something cold and hard.

'What am I holding?'

'A bar of one of the cells. Don't go away.'

I heard her moving off, and as she went the fear and misery left me, and I felt almost...normal.

'There's a light just ahead of me,' Cat said. 'Can you see it?' I peered. Saw a small circle, around ground level. 'The floor's given way here. Hang on, gotta be careful where I...I'm just going to...' She broke off. Then she said: 'There's something down there, something...huddled.'

'Huddled?'

'Holy smoke.'

'What?'

'It's a boy.'

5

'Hey, you down there,' Cat called. 'Turn that torch off, it's in my eyes!'

The little light went out. The darkness was total again.

Then she was firing questions into the hole she must have been kneeling or standing beside. Questions that got no answers.

'Is he just quiet,' I asked, 'or have I gone deaf all of a sudden?'

'He's looking up at me, not saying a word,' Cat said. 'Maybe he's in shock. He must have fallen in there, so that could be it. We've got to get him out. Hey, you! Boy! I'm going for help, all right?'

When she said this I felt suddenly happy, like the sun had burst through storm clouds or something. But it wasn't a feeling of mine, I knew that now.

Now green eyes were floating back to me at head height.

'What's your name?' Cat asked as she drew near.

'Me?' I said.

'No, the sixteen other people here in the dark with us.'

'Dax.'

'Dax? What's it short for?'

'It's short for nothing.'

'OK, Nothing, take my hand.'

'What? No. Get off.'

She grabbed the one gripping the bar and pulled it away. Then I was stumbling over the uneven floor, hand in hand with her like a little kid, my other hand in front of my face to ward off cobwebs, falling plaster, bats, and anything else I could imagine but not see.

'We're at the hole,' Cat said at last. 'Kneel down. But watch out. Seems firm enough round the edges, but we don't want to take any chances. Talk to him.'

'Talk to him? What about?'

'It doesn't matter. Anything, the weather, your first memory, why bumblebees fly backwards, up to you, I'm off.'

'No. Wait. You can't leave me here.'

'I have to. No one's going to know about this unless they're told.'

'Why don't I come with you? He's not going anywhere.'

As I said this, panic ripped through me so fast I

almost fell into the hole myself. Maybe Cat saw this, I don't know, but she said, 'Don't worry. I shouldn't be more than a day or two.'

'A *day* or two?'

Her laughter drifted into the darkness, and then it was just me, kneeling at the edge of a hole I couldn't see. I tried desperately not to think of the absolute nothing beneath me that probably went right down to the centre of the earth, and the hideous monsters advancing silently on all sides, reaching for me with bony fingers, keen to rip my lungs out.

To distract myself, I started talking.

'Hey, you down there. Why were you strolling around this ruin in the middle of the night?'

I waited. No answer.

'What, nothing to say for yourself?' I said.

Another wait. Still nothing.

Getting annoyed, I leaned over a little and yelled down.

'Listen, you think I want to sit here talking to myself in the dark? Gimme a grunt, gimme a song, gimme anything, just—'

That's when the edge of the hole gave way.

Down I went, head first, feet last. It wasn't a huge drop, but it might have ended painfully if I hadn't landed on the boy. He must have been pretty winded, but he managed to ask if I was all right.

'So you *do* speak,' I said, rolling into a sitting position.

I heard a gasp. Not a 'you fell on me and crushed the air out of me' type gasp. A gasp of wonder.

'You can *hear* me?' he said.

'Course I can hear you, I...'

I stopped because I'd realised that I hadn't heard a voice at all. Not with my ears. I stared. Stared at nothing, on account of the absolute coalmine-at-night-in-sunglasses style darkness.

'You spoke without using your *voice*?' I asked.

'So few people can pick me up,' he replied – in my head again, not my ears. 'It's almost a year since the last one. Jimmy. He went to foster parents.'

'But why don't you just *speak*?' I said.

'I don't do that,' he said, still in my head. 'Never have.'

'You mean you can't?'

'I mean I don't. Who was the girl with the eyes?'

'She calls herself Cat. She can see in the dark.'

'You two came looking for me?'

'Yes. Didn't know it was you till we got here, though.'

'I was getting desperate. Thought I'd be down here till I rotted.'

'That must be what I felt.'

'Sorry?'

'The desperation.'

'You felt it?'

43

'I felt something. Misery...fear...'

'Wow. That never happened before, or if it did I didn't know about it.'

'Why are you in this part of the building?' I asked.

'I was running away.'

'Running away? To *here*?'

'From the school. I tried telling Mrs Gardhouse I didn't want to come here, but like almost everyone else she couldn't hear me.'

'Mrs Gardhouse?'

'Director of the orphanage.'

'Couldn't you have written her a note?'

'We were in the car. I couldn't write in the car, and I didn't try before because I didn't know they were sending me here till I was almost on my way.'

'If you wanted to do a runner,' I said, 'the front door might have been a good place to start.'

'I was trying to find another way out. Didn't want to risk being seen.'

'You wouldn't have been if not for Cat's eyes. What's your name?'

'My name?'

'It's all right, don't tell me. I don't care anyway.

I'll call you Speechless.'

'Speechless?'

'Yeah. Suits you down to the ground – literally, in this hole.'

Suddenly a mad giggle ran around inside my head.

'Speechless!' the giggler said, also in my head. 'Brilliant!'

'Brilliant? What is?'

'Speechless. That's the first time I've laughed since I got here!'

6

The boy was quite chatty once you got past the lack of lip work. The chat helped the time pass, but I was glad when I eventually heard voices with my ears, up above.

'Over there. Careful where you walk. Follow me.' That was Cat.

'Turn your torch on.' That was me, to my holemate.

He ran the little torch's beam around the top of the hole as Cat approached with whoever she'd brought.

'Oh, where's he *gone*?' I heard her say. 'I told him to stay here.'

'Down the hole!' I shouted.

A torch, a proper torch, appeared over the edge and blinded us.

'What are you doing down there?' Cat yelled.

'I thought Speechless might be glad of the company,' I replied.

Another mad giggle jogged round my head with its arms in the air like my skull was an arena. Then a second voice spoke from up top.

'Oh, it's him. I knew he was trouble the moment I saw him. Should have stuck to my guns and left him on the step.'

My pal Doc Withering.

There was another man too. Mr Banner, the miserable cove who put the mattress in Cell 10 for me. He threw down a rope ladder whose unravelling end smacked me on the shoulder. I told Speechless to go up first. When we were both on the surface we could see (by torchlight and Cat's eyes) that our three rescuers were all in dressing gowns. Withering's hair stood up like he'd been having a chat with a wind machine.

'I imagine you're one of my students,' he said to Speechless.

'He doesn't speak,' I told him. 'But yes, he's one of yours.'

'What do you mean, doesn't speak?'

'I mean he doesn't speak. Not sure how else to put it really.'

'Why doesn't he?'

'Ask him, not me. Not that he'll tell you, on account of...guess what.'

'So you didn't find out what he's doing in this part of the building?' Cat asked me.

I glanced at the boy. 'He couldn't sleep and got lost,' I said.

'Thanks,' he said, in my head.

'There'd be no danger of things like this happening if you put barriers up to stop people going where they shouldn't,' I told the Doc.

'Well I *imagined*,' he replied (kind of frostily, I thought), 'that a notice in big letters bearing the warning that it's dangerous to go beyond that point would have been sufficient. Clearly I was wrong. When you've left us in the morning I'll jump to it and ensure that something less navigable is erected there.'

'You didn't say you were leaving,' a voice said in my head.

'It didn't come up,' I answered.

'Why did you say that?' Withering asked me.

'Say what?'

'"It didn't come up."'

'I was answering him. I can hear him, but no one else can.'

'I heard him,' said Cat.

Speechless stared at her. 'You can hear me?'

'Yes,' she said, obviously as amazed as he was.

'Are you telling me,' the Doc said to Cat and me, 'that this boy can communicate with you two *mentally*?'

'I thought it was just me,' I said. 'But yes.'

He was still trying to get his lofty head round that when Cat turned to him and said, 'What's this about Dax leaving?'

'Dax?' he asked her.

'Him,' said Cat.

He pulled a weary face, like he was so sick of explaining this. 'We have forty places at Scragmoor. Forty places for forty students. But thanks to an error that's not of our making forty-*one* have turned up – he being the forty-first, which makes him surplus to requirements. Out of the kindness of my heart I gave him a mattress for the night – a mattress to which I suggest he returns post-haste unless he wants to be put out into the night after all.'

'But Dad, he *led* me here!' Cat said. 'Without Dax we might not have found this boy till it was too late!'

I stared at her. 'Dad? This...he's...?'

49

'My father. Didn't I say?'

'No. I thought you were one of the students.'

'I am one of the students.'

I eyed the two of them, standing together in the green light of her eyes and the torchlight. They were both tall, but that was the only thing they had in common, physically.

'A student and his daughter?' I said.

'Adopted daughter.'

'Adopted. Well, at least you're not a blood relative. The rest's bad enough without that.'

'Dad,' Cat said, 'you have to let him stay, if only out of gratitude.'

'My gratitude,' the Doc replied stiffly, 'will be confined to a simple word of thanks. Forty students, forty places, end of story.'

'But you're in charge! You can do what you like!'

He scowled down at her. 'I can*not* do what I like. I'm an employee. There are rules which I, like everyone else, must abide by.'

'So he can stay?' Cat said.

'Cat, my dear,' he replied, 'this appears to be one of those "read my lips" moments.'

He aimed the torch in his hand at his mouth, and said, very slowly, 'This boy...cannot...*stay*!'

'So you'll sleep on it?' said Cat, all glowing green eyes.

Her father gave a sort of strangled growl and said to Speechless and me, 'You two, back to your cells. And you to yours, Cat. Now!'

7

Marcus, the other boy in our cell, hadn't woken up the whole time we'd been gone, so he had no idea what had happened. He woke when the screaming started, though.

So did I.

So did Speechless.

Most of the screams were coming from boys in other cells, but they were also coming from ours.

From Marcus.

We left him to it and went outside with our hands over our ears. Others had the same idea. The screamers were in three other cells as well as ours. Four boys sitting up in their bunks yelling their heads off. We could hear other screams too, distant ones, from the girls' cells.

'Anybody read them nasty bedtime stories?' someone said.

The screams had just started to die away when a gang of adults appeared in dressing gowns, again including Dr Withering, but not Mr Banner.

'You know you said you could still hear screams in the cells?' I said to the Doc.

'I didn't mean *these* cells,' he snapped.

When the screaming finally stopped, the boys who'd been doing it looked kind of embarrassed. At first, none of them wanted to talk about what had set them off, but when the adults had gone it started to trickle out that they'd all had a nightmare – the *same* nightmare – of a hideous monster reaching for them. One of the boys drew a picture of the monster and the others said, 'Yes! That's it! That's it!'

It was Speechless who identified the type of creature it was, though I was the only one to hear him say, 'Looks like a gargoyle.'

I agreed. 'Like the one on the roof.'

'There's a gargoyle on the roof?'

'Yeh. Noticed it as I arrived.'

'A gargoyle on a prison is pretty unusual,' he said.

'It might be unusual,' I said, 'but it sure wasn't pretty.'

In the morning there was a lot of talk about the screaming and the nightmare, especially as the girl screamers had also dreamed of a gargoyle. I didn't want to get into any of that myself, or meet the other kids, and when they went to breakfast I snuck to the kitchen to see if I could find something there. I could, because there was a cook there today – Mrs Beverage – and when I told her I was leaving she said, 'Don't blame you, sunshine. Last place I'd be too if there was work anyplace else on the moor.'

'You don't like it here then?'

'Like it? My great-granddaddy was hanged here.'

'Why, what did he do?'

'He stole a lamb. The family was hungry, and they

strung him up for it. How's that muffin?'

When I was all done I went back to the cell for my suitcase. Speechless was there already, sitting on the lower bunk, reading.

'How are you getting home?' he asked.

'Train, if I can get to a station and there's someone to drive me there.'

'He can drive us both then.'

I shrugged and headed out with my case. He followed, with his.

Down in the entrance hall I started towards Dr Withering's office, but he didn't go with me.

'Aren't you coming?' I called back.

'I haven't told anyone I'm leaving.'

'Well maybe you should.'

'No. They might try and stop me.'

'If the Doc finds us a driver he'll know anyway.'

'Maybe I should walk then.'

'Not advisable. A man was found dead out on the moor recently. Fell down something. Still, you have experience of falling down things...'

'All right, I'll tell him.'

We went to the door with 'Dr Withering' on it. I

knocked. No answer. I tried the door handle. The door opened. I looked in. Saw a big desk, couple of chairs, a filing cabinet, a hat stand, a map of the moor that covered most of one wall. No human life, or even insect.

'May I help you?' a voice said behind us.

I turned. Looked at a man's chest. Then I raised my eyes to the face just under the ceiling.

'Ready to go, Doc,' I said.

'Go?'

'To the station. You said you'd get someone to drive me.'

'I believe I said I'd see if there was someone *available*. Sadly, there isn't. Lessons start today and everyone's busy. Why are there two of you with cases?'

'He's leaving too.'

'You're leaving?' he said to Speechless. Speechless nodded but had trouble meeting his eye – not only because it was so far above the ground. 'You can't leave just like that. Your people assigned your care to us. We'd be failing in our duty if we allowed you to walk out without alternative arrangements being put in place.'

'He's right,' I said. 'You can't go.'

'You are,' Speechless said – inside my head, of course.

'Yeah, but I shouldn't be here anyway according to him.'

'Are you both talking?' the Doc asked. I half shrugged a yes. 'You could have quite a future with that,' he said to Speechless.

'Doing what?'

'He said, "Doing what?"' I told the Doc.

'I'm not sure yet, but whatever it turns out to be he's

in the right place to fulfil his potential. He'll get all the encouragement he needs at Scragmoor.'

'There you are,' I said to Speechless. 'You'll fit in here. It's different for me. I don't belong.'

He stuck his jaw out. 'If you're going, I'm going.'

'No, look,' I said. 'I have to, you don't. That's the way it is, right, Doc?'

'Doctor,' said Withering.

'Neither of you is going anywhere,' said another voice.

It was Cat. Her eyes weren't glowing now.

'Keep out of this, please, Cat,' her dad said.

'I will not keep out of it,' she replied. 'You promised to think about letting Dax stay.'

'I promised no such thing.'

'You said you'd sleep on it.'

'No, you said that. But if I *had* slept on it, nothing would have changed. There's simply no place for him here.'

'You know, that message is starting to sink in,' I said. 'But I still need a driver to speed me on my way, and if you lend me a hat I could throw it in the air with joy as I go.'

'I'll drive you myself if need be,' the Doc said coldly.

'Daddy,' said Cat in a silky sort of way, 'this boy' – she meant Speechless – 'can only make himself heard through Dax or me. How will he communicate with anyone without Dax here?'

'Well…through you, I suppose.'

'Girls and boys don't always do the same things, so I won't always be there when he has something to say. Dax could be.'

'I'm sure we'll find a way round that,' the Doc said gruffly.

Cat sighed. 'I didn't want to do this, but you leave me no choice.'

'No choice for what?'

'I'm calling in the debt.'

'Debt?'

'You owe me, Daddy, have you forgotten? Without me...'

She waved her hands to take in the entire building.

The Doc frowned. 'Now that's not fair, Cat,' he said.

'I know, but you brought me up to believe that debts should always be paid, and now's the time for you to repay this one.'

He stared at her for a few seconds, then groaned. 'Oh, wretched girl, *wretched* girl!'

'Sorry,' said Cat. 'But do this, let Dax stay, and we're quits.'

I decided that it was time for me to stick an oar in. 'Whatever's going on here,' I said to the Doc, 'don't give in to her. I'm out of here, OK?'

He turned to me and gave me a Withering glare.

'I'd be doing you a favour by sending you away, would I?'

'Absolutely. Biggest ever. I'll miss our little chats,

but we all have to make sacrifices.'

'Do you have that piece of paper handy?'

'What piece of paper?'

'The official acceptance you showed me yesterday.'

'Yeah, somewhere.'

I rummaged, found it, handed it over.

'You want to tear it up?' I asked. 'Put a cross through it? Write "Return to Sender, Boy Unknown", something like that?'

'I want to study it.' He read the paper through, slowly, right to the end, then said, 'It appears to be legitimate.'

'It was legitimate yesterday too,' I pointed out.

'Yes, but on due consideration...'

I felt suspicion narrow my eyes.

'Due consideration?'

'Inconvenient as it is, I don't think I have a choice in the matter. You'll have to stay.'

'No, no,' I said. 'Forty students, that's the intake, said so yourself more than once or twice. Speechless is staying – right, Speechless? – so you've still got your forty, no room for any more, great to meet you but I must be off.'

'You're going nowhere,' said the Doc.

'What?'

'You're an unwanted extra and an odd number, but we must squeeze you in somehow.' He shook the official document in my face. 'Signed and sealed, Forty-one. Official.'

I opened my mouth to protest, but nothing came out. Suddenly I was as speechless as Speechless, who was grinning like he'd just hit a scratchcard jackpot.

Cat nudged me with a shoulder. 'Hero 41,' she whispered.

'Hero?' I said. 'I had a bad dream and fell through a floor. I'm no hero.'

'I don't mean that.'

'What then?'

'You'll see.'

And she walked away, like a Cat that got the cream.

With me the cream.

So listen. Next time you feel a moan coming on about school feeling like prison think of Dax Daley, who really *was* in one. All right, it was an *ex*-prison, but it still felt pretty much like one that morning as I was herded along with the forty official students. The deputy head, Mr Soldoni, was leading us to another part of the building for some reason I'd missed because my head was in a whirl about still being there instead of in a car zooming towards liberty. I felt pretty much alone, but not as alone as I wanted to be. The boy who didn't speak out loud was keeping pace with me.

'You don't have to follow me everywhere I go,' I said to him.

'I'm not following you,' he answered, in my head.

'Not following me? Speechless, we're walking in *step*.'

He chuckled. 'Speechless. That kills me.'

'Glad to hear it. Get lost.'

He chuckled harder. 'I'm so glad I found you, Dax.'

'You didn't find me. I found you. Down a hole.'

'So you did. I don't think I thanked you for that.'

'Don't mention it. Ever. I don't want to be reminded of it.'

'Oh, it's so nice, you being able to hear me,' he said. 'So few can.'

'Cat Withering can. Follow her instead.'

I tried the odd skip to get out of step, but two paces later he was back in. Very frustrating.

We were shown into an enormous corner of the building that was even more ruined than the rest. The floor was bare paving stones lined with weeds. The walls rose to the clouds. No ceilings on the way, no roof at the top.

'Welcome to the North Wing of Scragmoor Jail!' boomed a voice.

Forty-one pairs of eyes looked to see where this came from: speakers on two of the walls.

'The North Wing,' the recorded voice went on, 'was where the most dangerous prisoners were kept. There were six storeys here, each one containing dozens of cells, but the floors have long since caved in or been removed for safety's sake.'

While the voice carried on telling us about this hollow

ruin and other parts of the place, Mr Soldoni went to stand beside a wooden platform and Dr Withering came in and climbed the steps to the platform. When the voice finally shut up, the Doc took a turn.

'Good morning, one and all!'

A few kids shouted 'Good morning!' back. I wasn't one of them.

He beamed around, and said, 'For those who don't already know, I'm Dr Withering, Head of Scragmoor Prime. I'm sure I'll get to know you all individually in due course, but for now let me just welcome you and assure you that in spite of its charms this will not be our regular assembly point.

I've asked you here in order to give you some idea of the character and scale of the building you'll be working and living in. Now,' he added after a small pause, 'I'm sure you'll be wondering why you, just you forty, have been selected to come to Scragmoor.'

'Forty-one,' I said, more loudly than I meant to.

Withering eyeballed me for a second, then carried on as if I didn't exist.

'Each of you possesses a rare gene – the Lomas Gene, named after its discoverer, Karlheinz Lomas. It's thought that with a little encouragement this gene will trigger abilities – powers, if you like – way above the norm, and that by bringing so many genetically advantaged youngsters together under one roof...not that this part of the building *has* a roof...'

Pause for laughter, which didn't come because he'd said something that had pricked up every single ear.

'...those abilities will reveal themselves where they might not in isolation. This seems to have been borne out already in a rather amusing way. We believe that the alarms and lights going wild during yesterday's welcome dinner was thanks to the simultaneous presence of so many Lomas Genes. With luck that won't happen again, but as yet very little can be predicted about the behaviour of the Gene, especially in quantity. That's why this school needed to be so far from what some like to think of as "civilisation".'

'Sir?'

A girl had thrown her hand in the air. Withering's smile shrank, and he frowned a little, like he didn't welcome interruption. But he let the girl speak.

'You said "powers"...' she began, and immediately dried up.

'I believe I did,' he said. 'You have a question?'

'Well yes, sort of. I mean...powers?'

'The geneticists tell us that each Lomas Gene hosts one power – just one – which will almost certainly be unusual and could be rather extraordinary. They can't say what that power will be in any individual case, but they're confident that you will all acquire one, sooner or later.'

A murmur had started to rumble around the huge ruined wing.

The Doc held up a hand, and the murmur fizzled.

'I was going to leave this to Mr Soldoni,' he said, pointing to his deputy below the platform, 'but as your interest seems to have been stirred...'

He paused, waited for the silence to develop an echo full of dropping pins, and leaned forward.

'Students of Scragmoor Prime,' he said, speaking very slowly for dramatic effect, 'each of you...is a superhero in the making.'

9

I don't think anyone listened too closely to Withering after that. I know I didn't, but not because I was thinking 'Wow, me, a superhero?' like most of the others seemed to be. Someone made a mistake when they put me on the list of kids to go to Scragmoor, which had to mean that I didn't have this Lomas Gene. Fine by me. What would I do with super powers? Hold the TV over my head? Listen to someone else's headphones with my super hearing? Jump over bungalows in a single bound? What possible use were such things in real life?

I felt eyes on me. I looked to my left. Cat Withering, watching me. She grinned. I glared. She'd called me Hero 41, which meant she already knew about this and thought it a huge joke that she'd got her old man to let me stay. Me, the only kid who wasn't going to have a power.

A minute later the Doc handed us over to Mr Soldoni, who led us out of the North Wing. Lots of excited chat as we followed. None from me. Cat caught me up. 'You don't look very pleased,' she said.

'What have I got to be pleased about?'

'Well...being here?'

'I don't *want* to be here. Didn't you catch that? Didn't you hear me tell that old buzzard that he'd be doing me a favour by putting me on a train?'

'Do you mind? That old buzzard's my dad.'

'You said it. How does it feel to be a superhero?'

She pulled a face. 'Superhero. I think that's stretching it a bit. But I'm not one yet anyway.'

'What about the glowing eyes? The seeing in the dark thing?'

'That's just a quirk. I've always had it. Nothing to do with the Gene.'

'But you've got that too?'

'Well, yes. That's how Dad got the job running this place.'

'Eh?'

'He'd been a school head before, quite a successful one. Turned around a failing secondary in a very run-down area. He was coming up for retirement when he heard he was on a shortlist of people who might be suitable to run Scragmoor Prime. Thought

71

he might be too old, but then they discovered that his daughter had the Gene and thought that with me as one of his students he would have a vested interest in making the place work.'

'Is that the debt you called in to get him to keep me here?'

'That's the one.'

'You should have saved it. Why did you want me to stay?'

'I was curious to know why you were so keen to leave. It's a pretty unique deal we have here.'

'Not for everyone,' I said.

Mr Soldoni led us through other parts of the building and out the front door, down the steps to the cobbled courtyard.

'The structure on your left was a stable block originally,' he said as we crossed the yard, 'though in Scragmoor's museum days it served as a tea room. There's a cabinet in there packed with artefacts and information about the jail for those of you who are interested in such things. Right now, though, we're going to that shed in the corner. You'll soon see what *that* was used for!'

'Dax, look up,' a voice said suddenly, in my head.

I glanced around. Speechless, of course. 'You still here?'

He grabbed my arm, and I stopped. Others walked round us.

'The roof,' he said. 'The gargoyle.'

I looked up. The gargoyle was staring down, just like yesterday when I arrived...like it was meant to do...except...

The sky was behind it, above it, so you couldn't see it clearly, but I could swear that its jaws were opening and closing, slowly, like it was stretching them to see if they worked. I brought my eyes down. There are some things you feel better not thinking about.

'You saw it, didn't you?' Speechless said.

'I *imagined* something.' I whispered that. People might wonder who I was talking to if they heard me.

'Oh yes? We both imagined the same thing then, did we?'

I shrugged. 'It happens.'

'And the two of us imagining the gargoyle moving has nothing to do with last night's screamers all having the same nightmare about it?'

I had no answer to that.

The shed in the corner was gloomy, and smelt of something you couldn't put your finger on and wouldn't want to. The walls were very rough, with drawings and photos and display boards fixed to them. In the middle of a cracked concrete floor there was an enormous trapdoor secured by heavy bolts, and high above the trapdoor there was a noose.

Yes, a noose.

And just to make sure we understood what the noose and trapdoor were for, on the back wall there was a sign in big letters.

HANGING SHED

Mr Soldoni laughed when he saw some of our expressions. 'Don't worry, we don't bring you here for misbehaving in class. But if you look on the boards you'll find information about some of the unfortunates who breathed their last in this shed. I know it's all very tragic and rather macabre, but the Head feels you should be left in no doubt as to what Scragmoor was before your day, and something of those who were resident here in less comfortable and privileged circumstances.'

There was a lot of interest in the pictures and info on the walls, and some (boys mainly) were quite excited about the noose and trapdoor, but a few looked uncomfortable, including a girl who asked if we could go now.

'Shortly,' Mr Soldoni told her. 'As soon as you've been introduced to... Ah, here they are!'

Eight adults – four men, four women, all smiling and waving – had come in. Two of each wore tracksuits. They went to the Hanging Shed sign and stood in a row in front of it.

'Where's Jack?' Mr Soldoni asked them.

A blonde woman with the smiliest face of all said, 'He went for a ride earlier. Promised to be back, but he doesn't seem to have much sense of direction, so that could be the last we see of him.'

The others laughed at this. Mr Soldoni just smiled.

'Students,' he said. 'Gather round and let me introduce you to...'

I forgot the names as soon as he said them, but I got used to them later on. The men were Mr Gladhusband, Mr Cosmo, Mr Ruffalo and Mr Kanwar. They were all tutors. Three of the women were also tutors – Mrs Page-Turner, Miss Niffenegger and Ms Samson – but the fourth, Miss Piper, the smiley blonde, was the school librarian.

'About half your lessons,' Mr Soldoni told us, 'will be in standard subjects: English, Maths, Geography, History and so on.' Groans all round. The staff's smiles broadened, like they were looking forward to torturing us. 'The rest will be dedicated to realising the Lomas Gene's potential, which is really why you're here, as Dr Withering told you. Four of your tutors – we think of them as your *super* tutors – will be helping you in that regard.'

He nodded at the four in tracksuits, who stepped forward, beaming.

'Ladies and gentlemen,' Mr Soldoni said to them. 'Off with those tracksuits!'

Mouths dropped open as the four tutors threw off their tracksuits, though what was underneath wasn't what you would expect a teacher to wear in a month of Mondays. Not underwear, not even bare skin, which was a relief (where would we have *looked*?). No. Other clothes. Very unusual clothes.

Outfits. Costumes.

Mr Gladhusband's was a neck-to-toe one-piece, bright green, a little saggy under the armpits, with a bad drawing of a beetle on his chest.

This would have seemed pretty wacky on anybody, but on Mr Gladhusband, whose gut flopped over his belt, it looked like he'd invented a whole new branch of crazy. The look wasn't improved by the woolly mask with waving tentacles that he pulled on.

Compared to his, Miss Niffenegger's outfit was almost normal. Black boiler suit with a purple sash. Even when she dabbed some purple stuff around her eyes she didn't look like an escaped loon.

Mr Cosmo was quite a short man, and what you might call wiry. His costume was dark blue with two red zigzags on the chest. He wore a little cape, also blue, also zigzagged, and put on a mask that only just covered his eyes.

The look that got the most gasps was Ms Samson's. She was quite a big woman – muscular, not fat, like she'd been working out since birth. You could tell how muscly she was because her blue and yellow costume was skin tight. I mean tight as *skin*. When she twirled with her arms in the air, at least half the eyes in the Hanging Room shot out on springs.

While we were still gulping and goggling at all this, Mr Soldoni told us that in these costumes Mr

Gladhusband was called Bugman, Mr Cosmo was The Sportsman, Miss Niffenegger was Marsha L'Art, and Ms Samson was known as Delilah.

But the best was yet to come.

'Bugman, The Sportsman, Marsha L'Art and Delilah,' Mr Soldoni said, 'were once...superheroes!'

Which almost brought the shed down.

That four?

Superheroes?

'You may laugh,' said Mr Soldoni, 'but a few years back Bugman, Marsha L'Art, The Sportsman and Delilah were out on the streets fighting crime and injustice wherever they found it.'

'We weren't *exactly* superheroes, Jim,' Mr Cosmo said.

'Well no, not exactly, but...well, why don't you explain?'

'Glad to. We were teachers,' Mr Cosmo told us. 'Ordinary teachers who started a superhero appreciation club, designing our own costumes and getting as fit as we could while we were at it. It was just a bit of a lark at first, venturing out onto the streets and acting all heroic for a giggle, until we found that a few none-too-bright dodgy types – carjackers, burglars and so on – took one look at us and hoofed it.'

'Which got us thinking,' Ms Samson chipped in, 'that maybe we could do some good dressed that way. So we started patrolling the streets for real.'

'We like to think we made a *bit* of difference,' said Mr Gladhusband, waggling his tentacles.

'Tell us about your individual skills,' Mr Soldoni said, like this was a TV interview.

'I was a PE teacher,' said Mr Cosmo. 'My favourite sporty activities were running, long jump and boxing. I employed all of these as The Sportsman.'

'I taught English,' said Miss Niffenegger, 'and I—'

'Don't tell us,' shouted a boy with floppy blond hair. 'You beat the crims with dictionaries!'

This feeble excuse for a joke went down a treat with some of the other boys, who rushed to him, hands up for a high-five. Slapping palms all around him, the boy looked as pleased as a porpoise until his eyes met mine. My expression must have told him what I thought of high-fivers.

'Miss Niffenegger?' Mr Soldoni said.

'English teacher,' she repeated. 'But in my free time I did a lot of martial arts, which came in handy in my costumed identity. I called myself Marsha L'Art because my first name's Marsha.' She beamed at us. 'Clever stuff, eh?'

'Mr Gladhusband,' said Mr Soldoni next.

'I trained as an entomologist before I became a biology teacher,' Mr Gladhusband told us. 'As I'm sure you know, an entomologist is someone who's nuts about insects. I never aspired to be another Spiderman, but I was certainly influenced by some of the characteristics of certain insects. I was quite a mover in those days.' He patted his bulging gut. 'Not so much now maybe.'

'And...Delilah?'

Ms Samson showed her teeth. 'I taught Geography and History, but turned out to have a talent for whirling round very fast and delivering a sucker punch as I came out of a spin.'

With this she twirled, arms in the air, then twirled again, and again, moving across the shed until she suddenly came over all dizzy, spun off course, and crashed into the arms of a man in black leathers who'd just come in.

'Ooh, sorry, Jack,' she said. 'I really *must* stop demonstrating that!'

'Demonstrate it any time you like with me, Dot,' the man said, putting her down. 'Hope I haven't missed much,' he said to Mr Soldoni. 'Took the Harley out on the moor and got lost. Do you know, there's hardly a signpost out there, and there's so much *of* it. Perhaps that's why it's called a moor.'

'This is Mr Toliver, everyone,' Mr Soldoni announced. 'Mr Toliver's our tame psychologist, the chap you go to if you have any worries or problems.'

'I prefer counsellor,' said the man in leathers. 'And are they allowed to call me Jack? Mr Toliver sounds like me dad.'

'Having just introduced four staffers by their hero names I can't really object if that's your preference,' Mr Soldoni said. 'We were about to hear how our costumed quartet became Scragmoor Prime's super tutors.'

'Like to hear that myself,' Mr Toliver said, flashing teeth so white they might have been sand-blasted. As he joined the others at the Hanging Shed sign I saw him give smiley Miss Piper a special look. She turned away like she didn't want to encourage him.

'Well-meaning as their intentions were,' Mr Soldoni said, getting back to what he wanted to tell us, 'Delilah, Bugman, The Sportsman and Marsha L'Art were eventually forced to hang up their capes, masks and what-have-yous because vigilantism is rather frowned upon by our law makers.'

'We were told to pack it in,' said Miss Niffenegger. 'So we stopped patrolling the streets in these oh-so-flattering outfits and went back to teaching during the day and watching telly in the evening, like normal people.'

'And some of us got fat as a result,' said Mr Gladhusband, patting his gut again.

'When the Scragmoor Prime concept was mooted, however,' Mr Soldoni went on, 'they were the ideal candidates for some of the classes the governors had in mind. These gentlemen and ladies might not be genetically blessed like all of you, but it's felt that they're more qualified than most to help you develop the abilities which it's believed will reveal themselves to you before long.'

He paused, then turned to one of the non-costumed teachers.

'Now Mrs Page-Turner here – who assures me that she's never been a superhero – will take you away for what might be called a get-to-know-you session. Rita, they're all yours!'

11

Back in the main building Mrs Page-Turner showed us into a long side room that looked like an old pub. It had a bar with empty shelves behind it, and a big open fireplace, and lots of tables and chairs. There were pens and sheets of paper on the tables.

'As you already know,' she told us (though I didn't), 'this is where you take your meals, but in the Jail's heyday it was the Infirmary, and when it became a museum it was refurbished as a restaurant-stroke-bar. We thought that rather than call it the dining hall or whatever, we would revert to the original name, which means that you'll be eating in...wait for it...the Infirmary! Find some seats, please. Anywhere you like.'

Most of the kids, bright-eyed with excitement, grabbed tables near her, but I found one as far away as possible. I was an extra student, an unwanted one, I didn't feel part of any of this, and didn't want to be.

When everyone was seated Mrs Page-Turner went to a whiteboard propped up on the bar.

'Now I realise,' she said, 'that none of you had met

before yesterday and that some of you are missing your friends, your homes and amenities and so on. Scragmoor might seem a pretty forbidding sort of place right now, but it's only a building. You'll make chums here soon and probably have the time of your lives because we – that is you – are going to do things that have never been done before, in any school. For now, though, and as a way of kicking things off, let's have a bit of fun.'

She printed some words at the top of the whiteboard.

WHAT WOULD YOUR CHOSEN SUPER POWER BE?

'That's the question I want you to answer,' Mrs Page-Turner said. 'Each of you possesses a gene which in the right environment (which hopefully is Scragmoor Prime) should give rise to something extraordinary. A few of you might find yourselves with the same ability, of course – the odds are very much against forty different powers going to forty students, but—'

'Forty-one if I'd been one of them,' I muttered.

Mrs Page-Turner broke off. 'Pardon me?'

I looked up. Her eyes were on me. So were everyone else's.

'What?' I said.

'I thought you said something.'

'No. Just thinking aloud. Too loud, obviously.'

'Well, we'd love to hear your thoughts.'

'I don't think you would,' I said.

'Why don't you stand up and introduce yourself? If we're all going to get to know one another, we could start with you.'

I groaned. 'Must I?'

'Oh, go on, you know you want to.'

'I don't. I really don't.'

'Well then...as a favour to me?'

I stood up and mumbled my name.

'Sorry, didn't catch that,' Mrs Page-Turner said.

'Dax Daley,' I said, louder.

'Dax Daley,' she repeated. 'Unusual.'

'Not to me.'

'Well, everyone. Allow me to introduce you to... Dax Daley.'

'Hi, Dax.'

'Hey, Dax.'

'How ya doing, Dax.'

These were some of the things shouted at me while I stood there feeling stupid.

'Can I sit down now?' I asked Mrs Page-Turner.

'Of course. Any idea what super power you'd like, Dax?'

'Invisibility would be pretty cool right now,' I said.

'That's one I'd quite like myself too, sometimes,' she said.

I sat down, low in my chair, avoiding all eyes, and Miss turned back to the others.

'It's unlikely that any of you will end up with your power of choice,' she said, 'but let your imaginations go for a minute. Put your name on the piece of paper in front of you, then write down the super power you would most *love* to have. Will you do that for me?'

Now I've never been into muscle-bound chisel-faced hunks zooming around in snazzy outfits, kerpowing villains, but here I was, with forty people as chuffed as tossed pancakes at the thought of being like that, who'd been told to choose a super power they would like. What was I supposed to do? Sit there with folded arms and my lower lip out like a shelf? That's what I felt like doing, but everyone had heard my name, loud and clear. If they knew just one person in this rotten excuse for a school it was Dax Daley. So, rather than risk drawing even more attention to myself, I wrote down the super power I'd most like after invisibility and printed my name at the top of the sheet.

When we were all done Miss collected the papers, and you should have seen the pride on some of those faces when she said, 'Thank you, heroes!' Then she leant against the bar flicking through the sheets, saying things like 'Some interesting aspirations here,' and 'Oh, I love that!', and chuckling here and there. She paused at one and glanced my way, but said nothing. 'A number of you have opted for the same power,' she said when she'd gone through them all, 'but that's only to be expected. I'll write them on the board and we can chat about them.'

She didn't say who picked which while printing the chosen super powers on the board, but you could tell in some cases when a little voice squeaked 'That's mine!' or people looked especially pleased with themselves. Here are some of the powers she copied out.

- SUPER STRENGTH
- TELESCOPIC VISION
- ABILITY TO RUN REALLY FAST
- BULLET-PROOFNESS
- THE POWER TO SPEL GOOD
- MIND LIKE A COMPUTER (QUICK AND SMART)
- POWER TO EAT PEAS WITHOUT PUKING
- WALL CLIMBING
- ABILITY TO CANCEL ENEMY SUPER POWERS
- POWER TO MAKE GARDEN GNOMES BE MY ARMY
- SUPER FLIGHT

    – FLIPPERS AND GILLS (TO SWIM WITH)
    – POWER TO ZAP ENEMIES WITH A FINGER

When she'd finished Mrs Page-Turner said, 'That's it, I think,' but then said, 'Oh, wait, there is one more,' and somehow (call it a super sense) I knew she'd been saving mine to last. I hunkered down in my seat and studied my table.

'Care to tell us what power you chose in the end, Dax?' Miss asked.

'My mind's a blank,' I said, hoping she'd leave it at that.

'I'll put it on the board then, shall I?' she said.

'No, it's OK, don't bother.'

'It's no bother – really.'

She took care that no one could see round her as she wrote my joke super power on the board, but said, 'Dax's choice is surely the greatest power of all!'

Then she stepped aside, and there it was, for everyone to see.

    – THE POWER NOT TO HAVE TO DO
      RUBBISH LIKE THIS

It got a few laughs, which wasn't so bad. But then the flop-head who made the pathetic joke and got high-fived in the Hanging Shed stuck his hand up.

'Miss!'

'Yes...erm?' Mrs Page-Turner said.

'Saxon Tull.'

Miss smiled. 'Dax Daley, Saxon Tull. What fine names you all have.'

'I'm just plain Jenny Jones,' one girl said.

'*Plain* Jenny Jones?' Mrs P-T said. 'Jenny Jones is a *great* name.'

Jenny Jones looked pleased to hear that.

Miss turned back to the boy. 'What is it, Saxon?'

He threw a big grin at me and said: 'Can I draw the super costume that someone with the power to never do rubbish like this might have?'

'Ooh, what an idea. I can't *imagine* what such a costume would look like!'

Tull went to the board on the bar and drew a weedy, scowling kid in a super costume with baggy underpants on the outside. On the chest he printed the letter D, twice.

'Initials of his super name,' he said, smirking at me.

'Surely his real name can't be his super name,' Miss said.

'Almost,' said Tull. 'His super name is Desperate Daley.'

A lot of kids stood up waving open hands as Tull headed back to his seat, smacking palm after palm. Just before he sat down, he waved at me.

I'd found my first enemy at Scragmoor Prime.

12

After the power wish list there was a lot of talk about what *actual* powers people might get. They were ordinary kids, nothing special about any of them till now, but they were starting to see themselves flying round the planet, shinning up skyscrapers, swinging between rooftops, all the usual fantasy stuff that made me laugh from the age of eight because it's so stupid.

'The rest of the morning will be getting-to-know-Scragmoor time,' Miss said when the chat about super powers started to go on too long. 'You're free to explore the building – up to a point. Now take note. It's a very *old* building, and some parts aren't safe to enter. You'll see signs warning you to keep out or go no further for one reason or another. Do *not* ignore such warnings.'

She glanced at me as she said this, don't ask me why.

'We can go anywhere else, though?' Saxon Tull asked.

'Anywhere except the offices and adult

accommodation, all of which are clearly marked. Now listen, everyone, listen!' She'd raised her voice as a roomful of chairs were scraped back. 'Reconvene here when the 12.30 lunch bell sounds, try not to get lost beforehand, and don't be too inquisitive about closed doors, dark staircases and cellars. We don't want to send out search-and-rescue teams on Day One. Day Two will be quite soon enough. Off with you now!'

As the other kids rushed to the door I saw Cat heading my way. 'Give you a guided tour if you like,' she said.

I stepped round her. 'I don't need a guide.'

In the entrance hall, everyone was laughing and trying to decide which way to go and who with. Saxon Tull was running upstairs followed by a bunch of boys who looked like they'd adopted him. Marcus Preedy was one of them.

I went out the front door and stood on the top step, looking across the courtyard towards the wall that surrounded the place, and the gateposts. There must have been gates between those posts once, I thought, or the prisoners would have walked. Would have been guards too, probably. No guards now, no gates, so I could leave any time I liked. If I did I might get lost on the moor, in the mist or fog, or the dark. I might stumble, twist my ankle. I might crawl for days with my twisted ankle and be too far from other humans for my yells to be heard. I might never be seen by another living soul till I was found, months from now, just bones and teeth, maybe a bit of hair.

But wasn't it better to take a shot at it than stay here?

I thought about my suitcase back in Cell 10. It contained my toothbrush, a few changes of clothes, but not much else. I could do without those things for a few days. I would miss food and drink, but maybe there'd be a lay-by with a van that sold stuff. My parents had given me a bit of money and I had it on me. Yes, I could manage. I'd get by. Go for it, Dax, I thought. Go for it.

I trotted down the steps. I was about a third of the way across the courtyard when I felt a drop of rain. I glanced up at the sky. Black cloud, right overhead. Ah well, a drop of rain, so what? While my gaze was up there it drifted across to the roof, and the gargoyle peering over the edge. It seemed to be leaning out further now, like it couldn't take its eyes off me.

'I won't be sorry to see the last of *you*,' I muttered, and carried on.

I was almost at the gateless gateposts when the black cloud split apart and rain started pelting down like a huge bucket had been tipped over. This wasn't going to be a shower. I'd be soaked to the skin, without a change of clothes. I looked for somewhere to shelter till it eased off. I didn't want to go back inside and risk rebumping into someone, but there were only three options out here. One was the corrugated roof over the cars and Jack Toliver's motorbike, but I could be seen from the school windows if I stood under that. Then there was the Hanging Shed, but once was enough in there. That left the ex-stable block. I ran across the courtyard more than half expecting its single door to be locked, but it wasn't. I pushed it open.

It wasn't very bright in there. There was a light switch, but not all of the bulbs in the roof worked, so I left the door open. Six compartments ran along the back wall – stalls for the horses that had once dossed and munched hay there. There were tables and chairs in a couple of the stalls, left over from the place's tea room days, and a board on the wall of the third stall along. I went to the board for something to look at while I waited for the rain to stop. Like the boards in the Hanging Shed it was full of sketches and photos of the jail as it was way back, and prisoners and staff from then. There were notes too, with the names of some of the people, and bits of info about them. I read some stuff about the warders. One of them – Harold Summerton – worked at the jail for forty-six years from the age of fourteen. Forty-six years in *this* place? Life sentence.

There was quite a bit about the executions too. In the seventeen hundreds there were over two hundred offences that carried the death penalty. Two hundred! As well as murder, crimes you could be hanged for included burglary, forgery and killing a sheep. There were photos of five hangmen, employed one after the other over a bunch of years. They didn't work at the jail full time but had other jobs outside and were called in when someone had to be topped. They were paid for each hanging. Two of the hangmen were father and son. There was something creepy about these two. The note beside their pictures said that when the son was a boy he helped his dad 'send the condemned on their way', and when Dad retired he took over. Nice little family sideline.

The other three hangmen wore black suits. Two of them, very stern-looking, could have been bank clerks. The other one, who wore a bowler hat as well as a suit, didn't look at all serious. His name was Collymore Spewdrift – what a name! – and he sported the biggest smile you ever saw that wasn't on a circus clown, and gave the camera a huge wink.

Collymore Spewdrift looked like one happy hangman. As well as the colossal grin and wink, there was another thing that made him stand out. According to the note beside his picture, his wife was condemned for burning a neighbour's cottage down, and he hanged her personally. I wondered if he was smiling and winking when he did *that* job.

I went to the door to see how the rain was doing. It was doing nicely, coming down harder than ever. I needed something else to look at. Fortunately, behind the door, along most of the end wall, there was a big glass display cabinet full of things from Scragmoor's prison days. Things like letters from families begging for mercy for their loved ones, work tools (planes, chisels, hammers), cloudy old bottles, jugs and jars, a big pair of kitchen scales. There was an old brown skull too, and more photos. One of the photos was of a gang of uniformed warders on the front steps, trying to look tough for the camera.

One big surprise was that in the centre of the cabinet there was a dolls' house and a bunch of toys. Toys! In a prison! But a note next to them cleared that up. They'd belonged to the two daughters and young

101

son of Bartholomew Hext, governor of the jail from 1887 to 1903. There was a picture of the kids with their dad. Governor Hext wore a suit and tie and had a pulpy sort of face and the bushiest sideburns ever. The toys included a spinning top, a little red and green steam train, a bowl of marbles, a Snakes & Ladders board, a doll with staring glass eyes, and a Noah's Ark surrounded by carved animals. The marbles were quite interesting. They were made of wood and weren't all shiny and perfect like the ones you see today, and some were coloured, with little pictures painted on them – by the governor's kids I reckoned because they weren't very good. They were kind of sweet, though, especially against some of the other stuff, like the old brown skull.

I was leaning against one of the glass panels when it jumped off its runner, leaving a gap just wide enough for a hand to wriggle through. Naturally, I reached in. I touched the spinning top and the Noah's Ark, and had just hooked a finger over the bowl of marbles to pull it closer when I heard a voice.

'What are you doing there?'

13

The voice was in my head, so I didn't really need to look to see who'd spoken, but I looked anyway. Speechless. In the doorway.

'What do I have to do to lose you?' I asked him.

'I was upstairs, saw you come in here.'

'Well now you can see me go out.'

I grabbed a handful of the wooden marbles and some of the Noah's Ark animals and dropped them in my pocket.

'That's thieving,' he said.

'So what are you going to do – send me to jail?'

I went to the door. It was raining harder than ever. But as I stood there something big smacked the cobbles right in front of me. Smacked and shattered. I jumped back, onto one of Speechless's feet. He yelped, out loud, not in my head, which proved he had a voice even if he didn't want to use it. Then we looked to see what had smacked and shattered. It was a big lump of stone. An ex-lump. Now it was in pieces.

'That building isn't *safe*,' I said.

He leaned out and looked up, against the rain. 'I don't think it came off the building,' he said. 'Didn't *fall* off anyway.'

I also leaned out, also looked up, and through the deluge saw, way, way up, the gargoyle, peering over the edge.

'You can't mean...'

I didn't finish because, distant as it was, and through pouring rain, it looked like the gargoyle was...chuckling.

I looked at Speechless. He raised his eyebrows at me.

'But it's a statue!' I said.

'It's a statue we need to take a closer look at it,' he said.

'Thanks, but I'm happy looking at it from down here. In fact I'd rather not even do that.'

'Aren't you curious to see if it really moves?'

'Speechless, it doesn't move. It can't. It. Is. A. *Statue*.'

'Yeah. And it's one that people have nightmares about. Several people all at once. That's not normal.'

'This *place* isn't normal,' I said.

'No. Agreed. There's a stairwell near the Head's office.'

'What about it?'

'It might go all the way to the roof.'

'I've seen it. I've also seen the sign that says don't use it.'

'Yes, but it doesn't block the way. Come on, Dax, let's take a look. Just one look. A little peek. It won't take long.'

Without waiting for an answer he jumped the

shattered lump of stone and ran across the courtyard and up the steps. I glanced towards the gateless gateposts. That was the way I *wanted* to go. But it was still raining too hard.

OK. Later. Or tomorrow.

I ran after Speechless.

Inside, a few kids stood about wondering where to explore next. We shook the rain off while they made up their minds, then snuck along to the stairwell near Withering's office. The steps on the other side of the UNSAFE ENTRY FORBIDDEN sign curved tightly round and were too narrow for two people to walk up side by side, so we tossed to decide who should go first. I lost, looked around to make sure we were alone, and climbed over the sign.

There were no lights on the way up – they probably used lanterns or candles in these stairs' heyday – which meant that it was soon pretty dark.

'Now would be a good time to produce that torch of yours,' I said.

'It would,' said Speechless. 'Pity I don't have it with me.'

Heading up into the ever-deepening darkness, I

trod more carefully at every turn in case the unsafe warning at the bottom meant what it said. The steps felt solid enough until we'd climbed about twenty of them, when a couple turned sort of spongy.

'Mind how you go here,' I said. 'These steps feel a bit—'

'Quiet!'

'I thought I was being.'

'I mean church-mouse quiet. Stop. Listen.'

I stopped, listened, and heard something way below us.

Footsteps.

'Someone following us?' I whispered.

'Why would anyone follow us up here?'

'Why don't you go down and ask them?'

'They've stopped,' Speechless said.

'Maybe they were an echo of ours,' I suggested.

'No. They were still coming after we stopped.'

'That's what echoes do. If they stopped right away they wouldn't be echoes.'

'I still don't think it was an echo. It might not even be a person.'

'What else would it be?'

'A ghost. Think of all the people who died here – at Scragmoor, not on these stairs. But maybe here too, who knows?'

'You're a real little ray of sunshine, aren't you?' I said.

'There they are again.'

He meant the footsteps.

'I really hope it isn't a ghost,' he said.

'You might wish it had been,' I said.

'What do you mean?'

'I mean it could be worse than a ghost.'

'Worse?'

'Might be an axe-wielding mass-murderer. Let's hope these stairs do go to the roof so we can jump up on it before he catches us and slices us into thin red pieces while grinning horribly.'

I shouldn't have said that because Speechless grabbed my sleeve from behind, shoved me against the wall, and scooted past me.

Now I was the one following him.

We carried on, up and up, round and round, as fast as we dared in the dark, on those old stairs, and the footsteps down below kept on coming. We still

had no idea if we could get to the roof, but we knew when we'd gone as far as we could because according to Speechless there was a sudden step shortage.

'That's really it?' I asked.

'I can't feel any more.' But then he said, 'Hang on, I think there's a ladder here.'

'A ladder?'

'Well, it's certainly a laddery sort of thing.'

I joined him on the top step, which was bigger

than the others, squarer, like a sort of platform, and groped around till I also felt something laddery. I put a foot on what felt like a rung, and my hands on others higher up, and started to climb. Yep, definitely a ladder.

There wasn't far to go. I realised this when I heard a mighty thud very close to my ears.

'What was that?' Speechless asked.

'My head hitting the ceiling.'

'Maybe it's the underside of the roof.'

'I think it's a trapdoor.'

'What makes you think that?'

'There's a bolt.'

'Well pull it. Or push it. But hurry, the footsteps are still coming and my knees have started to bang together.'

I waggled the bolt. It moved, just a bit. I waggled it some more.

'It's stiff,' I said.

'It's probably quite old,' said Speechless.

'Oh, you think?'

The bolt moved a little more. It wasn't keen, you could tell, but then it jerked the last bit, and the trapdoor swung down, cracked me on the side of the head, and I was dazzled by sudden light from above.

'We made it!' Speechless said.

I shinned up first, holding my poor battered head, with Speechless riding my heels. On the roof, his first thought was the same as mine, to reach down and haul up the trapdoor, put it between us and our follower. But to do that we'd have had to grow longer arms in a hurry and that was one of the many powers we didn't possess. So, leaving the trap hanging, we looked for somewhere to hide from the ghost, axeman or whatever. The roof was littered with chunks of stone like the one that hit the cobbles outside the stables. They were big chunks, but not big enough to hide behind. Speechless noticed this too.

'Well, at least it's stopped raining,' he said.

'Yes, a real blessing. Somewhere to hide would be another one.'

'There is one place.'

He nodded towards the gargoyle.

Its back was to us, long and broad, with a spine like a row of fat beads. Its wings were pulled in to its sides but looked lifelike enough to spread without warning if they hadn't been carved out of stone.

And that was the thing, of course. The wings, like the rest of it, were solid stone. It was a sculpture. A monster made to lean out from the roof and glare down at the prisoners who used to walk below, probably as a warning to watch their step. There was no chance of such a thing moving. Absolutely none. We really had imagined it.

The only trouble with hiding behind the gargoyle was that there was nothing there but an awfully long drop. It looked as if there might be a bit of room underneath it, though, if we really packed ourselves in. And we had to do it in a hurry. We could still hear the footsteps, and they sounded like they were almost up to the bottom rungs of the ladder now. Speechless and I glanced at each other, and nodded. Then we raced to the gargoyle, him to one side, me to the other, and dived beneath it, crashing together and huddling tightly between its ancient unspread wings hoping no part of us could be seen from the hole in the roof.

We were crouching there, holding our breath so as

not to be heard by whatever or whoever was following us, when something happened that we could have done without just then.

The gargoyle's wings...its ancient stone wings... fluttered.

14

Our first response was disbelief. Our second was skin-rippling horror. Rooftop gargoyles don't flutter their wings. But these had fluttered. They only fluttered once, but those flutters really gave us the willies, and the willies weren't helped much by the fact that we were crouching so close to the edge of the roof.

But because there wasn't a lot else to do just then other than have a quick mental breakdown, I peered under the wing on my side to see if we were still alone up there. We were, but only just. Two hands had gripped the edge of the trapdoor hole from below. Then the one the hands belonged to climbed out.

'Speechless,' I whispered.

'Don't talk to me, I'm hyperventilating.'

'We should get out from under here,' I said.

'Out? How can I when I'm frozen with terror?'

'Get over it. There's someone on the roof.'

'You mean the person, ghost or axe-murderer?'

'Yes.'

'Which?'

'Put a lid on the hyperventilation and take a gander.'

He looked under the wing on his side, and groaned. Then he slipped out. We both did. But I didn't rush away as fast as him. While he scampered to the trap hole I took another squint at the gargoyle, from a bit of distance this time.

It wasn't moving now. It was absolutely still. Which made me wonder if we'd imagined the wing thing like we'd imagined the other moves from the courtyard. If we had, how was it that even though it wasn't moving there was something about it that looked like it might do one or more of the following things any time:

1. *Throw its head back in a great howl.*
2. *Lift its wings to the skies.*
3. *Leap round to face me with drool flying out of its mouth.*
4. *Charge at me just as I was wetting myself.*
5. *Claw me to bits before I could say, 'Hey, let's talk about this'.*

I ran to the trap hole.

'What are you doing here?' I demanded.

'That's what he just asked,' Cat replied.

'And what did you tell him?'

'That I wanted to see where you were going.'

'Well why didn't you say?'

'When was I supposed to do that?'

'How about while you were following us?'

'And what would you have said if I had?'

'Stop following us.'

'Which is why I didn't. Why have you come up here?'

'We wanted a closer look at the gargoyle,' Speechless told her.

'Why?'

'To see if it really moved.'

'Really moved? It's made of stone. Things made of stone don't move. They can't, because...guess what. *They're made of stone!*'

'That's what I said,' I said. 'But this one does.'

'Does what?'

'Move.'

'You're mad,' Cat said, eyeing the gargoyle's bent back.

'OK, go and crouch under it,' I said.

'Why would I do that?'

'Because that's what we were doing when its wings fluttered.'

'Why were *you* doing that?'

'We thought someone was following us.'

'Someone was.'

'Yeah, but we didn't know it was you, did we?'

'Well no one's following me, so I don't need to hide.'

'You might want to now,' said Speechless. 'But not under the gargoyle.'

'What do you mean?'

He nodded towards it. Its wings were fluttering again.

Cat's mouth fell open. 'But...but...'

'Exactly,' I said.

'But it's lifeless. It's without life. Life is one of those things that stone creatures just cannot *have*.'

Now the gargoyle's wings lifted a little, and even from behind we could see that it was raising its head. When its knobbly old spine straightened up I think it's possible that three heads of human hair stood to attention too. The owners of the three heads might have spun around and scrambled down the trap hole right away if not for one thing.

We couldn't move.

Hair-raising horror kind of does that to you.

'Did you hear that?' said Speechless.

'Hear what?' I asked.

'It spoke. The gargoyle spoke.'

'I didn't hear anything.'

'Me neither,' said Cat.

'Well, I did. Inside my head.'

'What do you think it said?' I asked.

'"Who dares disturb me?" I think that's it anyway, it wasn't very clear.'

'Then I'll say it again,' said a deep, dark voice – not in his head this time, but in three pairs of ears – as the gargoyle stepped back from the edge of the roof and heaved itself slowly round.

Facing us, as it was now, I was able to examine it properly. I didn't *want* to examine it, but it was kind of hard not to as my eyes seemed to have lost the ability to blink. It had long talons instead of toes, and huge shoulders and arms, and flaring nostrils, and big pointed ears, and no hair. It also had jaws utterly *stuffed* with teeth that looked like they could rip the head off a stone lion at four paces.

And there was another thing. It only had one eye. A green one. There was an empty space where the other one should be.

A hollow black socket.

The green eye glared at us meanly – I mean *very* meanly – as the gargoyle leaned towards us, showed all its teeth, and growled, in an even deeper, darker voice: '*Who...dares...disturb me?*'

Suddenly we were no longer rooted to the spot. I'm not sure who was last down the hole in the roof, but it wasn't me.

15

At the bottom of the stairwell we separated. We didn't want to talk about what had happened, or even be reminded of it, and the best way to do that was to be nowhere near the two others who'd seen and heard the same things.

When the lunch bell went everyone headed for the Infirmary, where we found Mr Kanwar and Mrs Page-Turner waiting for us. They told us to form an orderly queue while the kitchen staff finished putting dishes and plates on the counter. While everyone else did just that, I went to the same table as before and sat down.

'Not joining us, Dax?' Mrs Page-Turner called.

'I'll wait for the feeding frenzy to die down a bit,' I said.

Hearing this, some of the kids about to join the queue also found seats. A couple of them nodded at me like I'd said something cool. I stayed put until the queue got short enough, then joined it, and the others who'd sat down did the same. The menu was baked potato with a choice of toppings, or chicken curry, or a veggie thing. I got spud and beans and carried my plate to my table. I was about halfway through eating when my chair lifted off the ground.

What?

You heard. It lifted off the ground.

It didn't lift far, but when a chair you're sitting on suddenly loses touch with the floor you kind of notice. I heard gasps from other parts of the room, but not because of my chair. Not *just* mine. Seven or eight other chairs were also hovering a little way above where they were meant to be. The kids perched on them were goggle-eyed, going 'Woh!' and 'What the...?', then one of them panicked and tipped sideways, gripped his table to stop himself falling, pulled it over as he went down, and ended up sprawling on the floor wearing a chicken curry face pack.

Others sprang from their floating chairs and stood well away from them or crouched beside them wondering what was going on. I was one of the crouchers. While crouching, I saw a girl with spiky black hair and glasses back away with a horrified expression. When all the hovering chairs suddenly fell with a clatter, she ran out of the room.

It wasn't just us kids who were startled by the furniture action. The tutors were too, but once they got over it they seemed more amused than anything.

'I think we might expect a fair bit more of this sort of thing in the days to come,' Mr Kanwar said to Mrs Page-Turner.

'Yes,' she said, and looked around. 'Anyone care to claim responsibility?'

No one did.

Those of us whose chairs had left the ground finished our meal standing, just in case, but they didn't move again. When we were done we were told to reassemble here in twenty minutes, which we did – all except the spiky-haired girl, I noticed. Mrs Page-Turner wasn't there twenty minutes later, but Mr Kanwar was, along with the four 'super tutors' – in civvies, I'm glad to say. Mr Kanwar told us we were going to be divided into four groups and each group would be taken to one of the communal cells in which dozens of prisoners used to be packed. These would be our regular classrooms, he said. Then he called ten names from a list in his hand – five girls, five boys – and asked them to go with Miss Niffenegger. After they'd left he called five more girls and five more boys and they went with Mr Gladhusband. Saxon Tull was in that group. I was very glad I wasn't going to be in the same class as him.

Speechless and Cat were among the ones still there, but Speechless went with the next ten, and Ms Samson. Cat gave me a 'Who's he gonna talk to there?' look. I shrugged a 'Search me'.

'If the rest of you are all here,' Mr Kanwar said when they'd gone, 'we won't need to call your names.' He did a head count. 'Ten. Can't argue with that. Toddle off with Mr Cosmo, would you please?'

The former cells the tutors led us all to stood around what Mr Cosmo told us was once an exercise yard for prisoners.

'We have to *exercise*?' someone said in horror.

'You're not prisoners,' said Mr Cosmo. 'But feel free if you wish.'

16

A row of floor to ceiling storage cupboards stood along the back wall of our classroom, but the other walls were bare. No posters, maps, paintings, anything. There were two windows, too high up to see anything out of other than a square of sky sliced by vertical bars.

There were ten desks and chairs, well spaced out and facing a bigger desk, and that was about it. Not the most exciting room to have to go to every day. Mr Cosmo must have felt the same, because he said, 'Our first objective was to make these rooms habitable. Decoration and adornment will come over time.'

He invited us to take our pick of desks. The eager beavers chose ones near the front. I picked one at the back. Then Mr Cosmo told us this wasn't going to be a lesson as such.

'What we want to do here,' he said, 'is see if anything unusual happens with so many of you gathered together in one space. There's no point in us just sitting here waiting, so we thought we'd run through a few exercises – don't worry, not very physical ones – in hope of encouraging your Gene to do its stuff. Let's start with you closing your eyes and emptying your minds.'

'My mind's already empty,' one boy said.

'Good, keep it that way. Eyes closed now, and those of you who aren't already empty-headed, please clear your minds.'

Once everyone settled down and eyes were closed the room fell silent. Mr Cosmo didn't close his eyes. I knew this because I ducked down so that others were between me and him. The silence didn't last. Inside of two minutes someone started snoring. Real snores, not jokey 'I'm so bored' ones.

'Was it something I said?' Mr Cosmo asked, craning his neck to identify the snorer, a boy sitting bolt upright with his head thrown back.

'Robbie couldn't sleep last night,' another boy said.

'You share a cell with him?'

'Yeh. He made sure I stayed awake too, going on and on about how he missed his bed at home.'

'So did I,' said a girl.

'Me too,' said another, 'but I was tired.'

'Well, we're not doing much that he can't afford to miss,' said Mr Cosmo, 'so let him slumber on. The rest of you, back to it, please, eyes closed, minds clear, see if anything happens.'

The closed eyes and empty minds thing went on for five more minutes, and nothing did happen, maybe because it wasn't easy to keep a clear mind with all the snoring.

'All right, we'll try something else,' Mr Cosmo said then.

The something else involved us getting up and stepping away from our desks. Robbie was woken up to join us in this.

'Stand on your right foot,' Mr Cosmo told us, 'and lift your left foot, and turn the heel of that foot out as far as you can, then count slowly to five and turn your left heel *in* as far as you can.'

'This is a *superhero* exercise?' someone asked.

'Not one of mine,' said Mr Cosmo. 'I'm just following instructions.'

'Whose?'

'My guess is some bright spark who knows as much about this as I do. But let's do it anyway.'

'You too, sir.'

'I don't have the Lomas Gene.'

'No, but you have to set an example.'

So he did the same exercise. A couple of kids lost their balance and had to start again, but when everyone had managed it, more or less, Mr C told us to switch feet and do the same thing the other way round. When we'd done this too he asked if anyone had felt anything. One girl said, 'Yes, stupid.'

'Oh, thanks, I'm sure,' said Mr Cosmo.

'Me, not you,' said the girl.

Next he got us to stand with our fists raised to see if any of us lifted off the ground. No one did.

'Just as well that one didn't work,' Mr Cosmo said. 'I'd hate anyone to shoot head-first through the ceiling.'

Then he got us to stare hard at small objects to try and move them. No one moved a thing. So he got us to try it with our eyes shut. There was a bit of excitement when a girl called Miyoko said the ruler on her desk was in a different place when she opened her eyes, but this turned out to be because the boy at the next desk moved it as a joke while they were closed.

If ever there was a rubbish set of exercises it was these, and it was pretty clear that Mr Cosmo thought so too, but he'd been told to run through them and a few others, which he did until Mr Soldoni came in with the spiky-haired girl who ran out of the Infirmary after the tables and chairs left the floor. She looked embarrassed.

'Excuse me interrupting,' Mr Soldoni said. 'This is Una. She was absent when Mr Kanwar called the rota, and missed her group.'

'But we have our ten,' Mr Cosmo said.

Mr Soldoni looked around. 'You have six boys.'

Mr Cosmo checked our faces and haircuts. 'So we have. How did that happen?'

'Oh, wait,' Mr Soldoni said. 'Dr Withering told me there'd been an administrative mix-up and an extra boy turned up yesterday.'

They both looked around like they expected the extra boy to confess. I sighed and stood up.

'That's me,' I said. 'This is your place,' I told the girl.

'Oh no,' she said, 'you were here first.'

'It's yours. Take it.'

I headed for the door.

'Where are you going?' Mr Soldoni asked.

'Dunno. Doesn't matter. I shouldn't be here.'

He jumped forward and got to the door before me.

'Wait. What's your name?'

'Dax.'

'Well, Dax, unless or until I hear otherwise, you're a Scragmoor student, and by hook or by crook we'll find a desk for you.'

'And a chair,' added Mr Cosmo. 'But in the meantime...'

He waved me forward, to his desk at the front of the class.

'You want me to sit there?' I asked.

'You'll be doing me a good turn,' he said. 'Force me to exercise my legs. I've become far too sedentary since I gave up superherodom.'

'Solved!' said Mr Soldoni. 'Take Mr Cosmo's place, Dax – as a temporary measure, of course – and Una, take yours at the desk he's kindly vacated.'

While Una sat down at my ex-desk, red with embarrassment, I went to Mr Cosmo's.

'Do I get to be in charge?' I asked him.

'If I can't hack it here,' he said, 'I'll put in a word for you.'

'I'll leave you to it then,' Mr Soldoni said, gripping the door handle.

He pulled the door towards him and his feet left the ground and floated halfway to the ceiling.

I'll say that again in case you missed it.

Mr Soldoni pulled the door towards him and his feet left the ground and floated halfway to the ceiling.

17

As coins and other things fell out of Mr Soldoni's pockets Una jumped up from the seat she'd just sat down in.

'Oh, no!' she cried.

A roomful of wide eyes turned from the upside-down deputy head to her.

'I was afraid of something like this,' she said. 'It's happened at home sometimes, but never as bad as this.'

'This isn't very dignified,' said Mr Soldoni, floating above the door handle. 'I wonder if someone would...?'

Mr Cosmo ran forward and grabbed him by the belt, but he'd just started to haul him down when Mr Soldoni's knees buckled and he came down anyway – right on top of Mr Cosmo.

'I'm so sorry!' Una wailed, almost in tears.

The teachers weren't upset, though. A bit rumpled, but not upset.

'This has happened at home, you say?' Mr Soldoni asked as he scrambled off Mr Cosmo.

'Not with people. Just objects, little things, and they only lifted a bit.'

'I heard that some chairs lifted off the ground in the Infirmary earlier,' said Mr Cosmo, also getting up. 'Was that your doing, by any chance?'

Una looked at the floor and wound one leg round the other. 'I didn't mean to do it, it just happened.'

Mr Soldoni laughed. 'It just happened! I'm guessing that being here with all these others, your little power is developing in ways that you might not have thought possible before.'

'Una,' said Mr Cosmo. 'You appear to be Scragmoor Prime's first superstar. That makes you quite a celebrity.'

Una looked up. Unwound her legs.

'Celebrity? Me?'

At this the other kids rushed to congratulate her. I stayed put behind Mr Cosmo's desk, but while everyone crowded round Una I heard a voice in my head.

'*The gargoyle wants us.*'

I saw Cat jump back from the scrum round Una. She looked my way, and from her expression I knew that she'd heard the same thing.

Just then the bell went.

'Short break now!' Mr Cosmo said. 'Back in |fifteen, people!'

Everyone piled out, taking Una with them. Cat and I followed, more slowly, and found, in the space where prisoners used to exercise, students from the second group patting a couple of theirs on the back. One of those being patted was Saxon Tull, who looked even more pleased with himself than earlier.

'Success?' Mr Soldoni asked Mr Gladhusband.

'Not half! These two really came up trumps. Tell them, Tamsin.'

'I shape-shifted,' Tamsin said, eyes big enough to pop out if she hiccupped.

'Into a chair!' said Mr Gladhusband. 'She became a *chair*! Curious thing is, we were one chair short – mine, as it happens.'

'You didn't sit on her, I hope,' said Mr Soldoni.

'I was tempted, but no.'

'We could have done with Tamsin in our class if she can turn herself into furniture,' said Mr Cosmo. 'We needed an extra desk.'

'Have you ever changed into anything before?' asked Ms Samson from the third group.

'No, Miss.'

'How did it feel?'

'I don't know. Weird. A bit...'

'Wooden?' said Miss Niffenegger from group one. This got a laugh.

'And what did you do?' Mr Soldoni asked Saxon Tull.

'Saxon grew muscles,' Mr Gladhusband said. '*Huge* muscles. If he'd been wearing a jacket the sleeves would have ripped apart.'

'I see no muscles,' I said. Tull gave me a sour look.

'They didn't last,' said Mr Gladhusband.

'There was quite a success in Mr Cosmo's group too,' said Mr Soldoni. 'Tell them, Una.'

While Una blushed madly and told everyone what she'd done, Cat and I looked for Speechless. We couldn't see him at first, but then a taller boy moved aside and we saw him hanging back, looking thoughtful. We went to him.

'You spoke to us from all the way over here?' Cat asked.

'Oh, you heard then,' he said. 'I made a special effort, but I wasn't sure it would work.'

'You said the gargoyle wants us.'

'Yes.'

'But he's even further away than we were.'

'I know. I don't think I ever picked up anybody that far away before.'

'He's not any kind of anybody,' I said. 'He's a piece of stone.'

'Stone that moves,' he said.

'You're sure you heard him say he wants to see us?' Cat asked.

'I didn't *hear* him exactly, I just sort of...got a feeling.'

'What do you think he wants?'

'I don't know, I was just sitting there and it came into my mind.'

'Overactive imagination,' I said.

He glared. 'Oh yeah? Like we both imagined him moving?'

'We'd better go up there later and see,' said Cat.

'Oh, I don't know about that,' I said.

She smirked. 'Scared of him, are we?'

'Scared? Nah. Just not in a hurry to make fresh eye-contact with him. Specially that eye.'

'I'm scared of him,' said Speechless, 'and I don't care who knows it.'

'Well, get over it,' said Cat. 'We're paying him another visit after lessons.'

18

There were two more lessons that afternoon. For our group it was English with Mrs Page-Turner followed by Maths with Mr Kanwar. Robbie the snorer didn't doze off in these, but I nearly did. When lessons were over we were free to do what we liked until dinner, and the three of us set off for the stairwell to the roof. On the way, Cat asked Speechless how he managed in class, not speaking out loud or into other heads.

'If I have a question or have to answer one I write it down,' he said.

He pulled out a little pad he said he always carried, and showed us some things he'd written.

'That's the most amazing handwriting I ever saw,' said Cat.

That went for me too. You'd never have guessed it was the work of a kid.

Passing a half-open door, we saw Miss Piper slotting books onto shelves. Unfortunately she also saw us.

'Hello!' she cried. 'Come to take a decko at our little library?'

'No,' I said, 'we're just—'

'Oh, do – *please.*'

She opened the door further, which didn't leave us a whole lot of choice. We went in, and found that she wasn't alone.

'Whatcher!' Mr Gladhusband said, arms full of books.

'Mr Gladhusband's helping me populate the shelves,' Miss Piper explained. 'I should have got everything sorted before the school opened, but never let it be said that I turn prospective readers away.'

The library wasn't very big, but it was brighter than any room I'd seen so far. The walls were painted pale yellow, like soft sunshine, with cheerful posters on them, and there were a couple of vases of flowers, and a desk with a computer on it, and shelves, of course, lots of shelves, half loaded, and there were more books piled on the floor.

'This used to be known as The Warders' Room,' Miss Piper told us. 'With a name like that, I suppose we should have kept it for the tutors to spill their morning coffee in, but I got first dibs, ha-ha, so it's mine, all mine!' She gave a funny-fiendish little laugh that you couldn't help smiling at. 'I'll be putting the hours on the door soon,' she added.

'You should put the century on the door too,' I said. 'The last one. No one reads books any more.'

'Now that is simply not *true*,' she said. 'You *cannot* beat a good book.'

'Can if you got a good stick,' I said.

'Ignore him, he's a boy,' said Cat.

'So am I and I read books,' said Speechless, but as Cat and I were the only ones who could hear him he might as well have saved his...whatever.

'Maris,' said Mr Gladhusband, 'where do the History of Scragmoor books go?'

'I thought we might create a special section for those,' she answered.

'There can't be many books about this dump,' I said.

'Not many,' she said, 'but enough for a small specialised section. Some of the students might be interested in reading up on it.'

'Not this one,' I said, and went out.

Cat and Speechless followed a few seconds later. As we walked away Cat said, 'Did you see the way he looked at her?'

'Who?' I asked.

'Mr Gladhusband.'

'No. How was he looking at her?'

'Like his eyes were melting.'

'Well, if he's sweet on her he'd better get in line,' I said.

They both gaped at me. 'You mean *you*?' said Speechless.

'Me? Get off, she's an old woman, thirty at least. No, Mr Toliver. Jack. He's younger than the rest, with better skin, hair, teeth. Those two are made for each other.'

We managed to make it to the stairwell without meeting anyone else, and hopped into it. Cat took the lead, her green eyeglow lighting the way, me next, then Speechless, this time with his little torch.

On the platform at the top, Cat stepped aside for me to shin up the ladder and open the trapdoor, like it was my job or something. I climbed out onto the roof and looked towards the gargoyle. He didn't seem to have moved since before, and he didn't move now at first, but then, as the others joined me, he turned round and fixed us with his one mean eye.

'You came,' he said in that deep dark growly voice of his.

'We thought you wanted us,' said Speechless.

'He did,' I said. 'I only came along 'cos I was told to. But if you don't...'

I turned to go.

'Stop!' the gargoyle said. I stopped. 'I do want you.'

'Curses,' I said.

'I don't understand,' said Cat. 'How can you speak? Move?'

'I've wondered that myself,' he replied. 'There seems to be something in the air. Something new. I feel it seeping into me...softening the stone.'

Six eyes looked at six others. The gargoyle's wasn't among them.

'What did you want us for?' asked Speechless.

'He won't be able to hear you,' I said.

'I have a feeling he will,' he said.

'I can hear him,' said the gargoyle.

'Well, that's three of us,' I said. 'Two flesh-and-bloods, one stone.'

'Come closer,' the gargoyle said.

None of us was very keen on this idea, but when Cat took a couple of steps forward, Speechless and I felt we'd better do the same.

'Why do you want to see us?' Cat asked.

'To inform you of something I recalled during the afternoon,' he said.

'Oh yes?'

'All the time I've been up here,' the gargoyle said, 'all these years – I'm not sure how many – I've been sad and not known why. Now I do.'

He paused, like he wanted to be asked why he'd been so sad. I looked away. So did Speechless. We didn't care.

'Why have you been so sad?' Cat asked.

He pointed at his empty eye socket. 'I've been missing this.'

'But there's nothing there.'

'It's what *was* there that I've missed,' he said.

'You mean an eye.'

'I mean the best eye in the world. My pride and joy.

I loved that eye more than life itself.'

Speechless and I glanced at one another. The glance said, *We're on the roof of an old jail listening to a stone gargoyle tell us he was once in love with an eye that he no longer has, someone up here's crazy, I wonder who?*

19

'This fantastic missing eye,' Cat said to the gargoyle. 'You only remembered it today?'

He nodded. 'All in a rush, just like that.'

'So what happened to it?'

'I don't know.'

'You don't know where your own eye went?'

'I can't remember. All I know is that it's gone and I want it back.'

'Well don't look at us,' I said.

'But I am,' he said. 'You three are going to find it for me.'

'You want *us* to find your eye?' said Speechless. 'Him, her and me?'

'I do,' said the gargoyle. 'In fact' – he reared up suddenly, towering over us, all teeth and eye and flaring wings – 'I *insist*.'

Cat was the first to find her voice after this announcement.

'You know, we'd love to help you,' she said. 'We really would, especially me, because I have a really soft spot for gargoyles. But we've only just started here, and we're going to be kind of tied up with stuff. There won't be a huge amount of time to do things like eye-finding for a while.'

The gargoyle, still in towering-over-us mode, glared down with his mean green eye.

'You'll make time,' he growled.

'Course we will,' said Cat. 'That's what I meant.'

'Hang on a tick,' I said, finding my voice too. 'This is insane – no offence, Mr Gargoyle – but if you don't know where your eye is and we don't either, where would we look for it?'

'That's for you to decide,' he replied.

I glared at Speechless. 'Next time you get a feeling that something made of stone wants to see us, keep it to yourself, will you?'

'Ooh,' said the gargoyle suddenly.

'Ooh?' said Cat.

'Another one's coming.'

'Another what?'

'Memory.' Then he laughed. 'I used to be human!'

'What?'

'Human! Me! What a thing to forget!'

'You can't have been human looking like that,' said Cat.

He stopped laughing, and glared again.

'Well obviously I didn't look like this *then*, did I?'

'All right, but how could you have turned from flesh, blood and all the other soft stuff to solid stone?'

The gargoyle sank down to normal level, and said, 'That has yet to come back to me. My mind, like my body, has only just begun to...' He broke off, then said, 'Oh-ho, something else,' and his eye widened as far as it could without popping out of his head. 'I was a taker of lives!' he said in wonder.

'A what?' asked one of us.

'A two-eyed life-taking man!'

'You mean as in...murderer?'

'I took many lives. Many, *many* lives.' He sounded quite proud of this.

'Oh,' said Cat. 'Well, it's good to know you did something worthwhile.'

She turned to go. So did Speechless. So did I.

'You have twenty-four hours,' the gargoyle said.

We paused. 'What for?' I asked.

'To return my eye to me.'

'But we've no idea where it's got to,' said Cat.

'Then you'd better *get* an idea, hadn't you? Because if I was a life-taking *man*, imagine – just *imagine* – what I might do as a gargoyle.'

'Is that a threat?'

'It is,' he growled.

'Oh. Right.'

'What if we can't find it?' asked Speechless.

'Then I shall turn you to stone, as I've been stone these many long years.'

'You could do that?'

'Oh, yes. No problem. And then I'll set you out there on the desolate moor, where you'll be at the mercy of the elements, cowed by storm, soaked by the heaviest rains, struck by lightning, blanketed by snow, shrouded by the thickest fogs, unmoving and miserable yet conscious through all eternity.'

'Dramatic sort, aren't you?' said Speechless.

'Listen,' I said to the gargoyle. 'Your eye could be just *anywhere*.'

'It could indeed. And as twenty-four hours will just *race* by I suggest you start looking for it without delay.'

'Twenty-four hours is nothing in a huge place like this,' Cat said.

The gargoyle looked over our heads, like he was thinking this over. Then he nodded. 'Very well, I'll be generous. Forty-eight hours. But if my favourite eye isn't back in place by the end of that time...'

'You'll turn us to stone,' I said.

'I will.'

'And put us out on the desolate moor,' said Cat.

'Correct.'

'At the mercy of the elements and so on,' said Speechless.

'For all eternity,' said the gargoyle.

With this he turned his back on us, leant out over the edge of the roof, and once again became cold, hard, unmoving stone.

2

Rebolting the trapdoor would have left us in pitch darkness if not for Cat's eyes, which immediately started glowing. 'Maybe he'll settle for one of yours,' I said to her. 'The colour's about right.'

She jumped down the first stairs. I went next. Speechless, waving his little torch behind me, said, 'That stuff he said up there about something new in the air, seeping into him, softening the stone...'

'What about it?'

'It's us. Has to be.'

'Us?'

'Students. A whole bunch of Lomas Genes under his roof and he comes to life after who-knows-how-long of being solid stone? Too much of a coincidence for it not to be. And hey, last night. Maybe his wakening image filled a few dozing heads down in the bedcells.'

'The nightmare?'

'The *shared* nightmare.'

'Well whatever else,' said Cat from below, 'I can't believe he was human once.'

'I can't believe any of this,' I said. 'Living gargoyles, super powers, me still here...'

We were about three-quarters of the way down when everything suddenly got brighter in front of me. Not hugely bright, but bright enough to see by – and green, like the glow from Cat's eyes.

'Where's that light coming from?' asked Speechless.

'You tell me,' I said, glancing back, and up.

He squawked and dropped his torch, which immediately died.

'Your eyes!' he said. 'It's coming from them!'

'What? What are you talking about? I...'

I stopped because when I moved my head the green light moved with it, and I could see clearly, even though his torch had snuffed it.

'What's going on?' Cat demanded, coming back up.

I looked down and she gasped and fell against the wall. I could see her as clear as day – green day – and not by the light of *her* eyes. I held my hand up. It was green, illuminated by *my* eyes.

'You know what this means, don't you?' Cat said. 'Your power's kicking in.'

'No,' I said.
'Impossible.
I haven't got the
Gene. I'm here
by mistake.
Anyway, you said it yourself, seeing in the dark isn't a power.'

'It isn't for me. It's something I've always been able to do. But you haven't. Sorry, Dax, like it or not, you have the Lomas Gene.'

'If he has,' said Speechless, 'it's not working overtime.'

The green light had faded and we were back to the glow from Cat's eyes.

'Can we get out of here?' I asked.

We carried on down, not saying a word, me especially. I had nothing to say. I didn't even know what to *think*.

And to cap everything off, at the bottom, just as we're hoisting our legs over the UNSAFE ENTRY FORBIDDEN sign, who should stroll by but Doc Withering. Who scowled heavily when he saw us.

'What were you three doing in there?' he demanded.

'We got lost,' Cat told him.

'Lost? What you appear to have lost is the ability to *read*. Explain.'

'We only went a little bit round the bend,' she told him.

'Speak for yourself,' I said.

'I expect you to be more responsible than this, Cat,' the Doc said. 'Some of you might not be' – he glared at me – 'but you, certainly.'

She looked at her feet. 'Sorry, Dad.'

'Very well, we'll say no more about it. But I *sincerely* hope that nothing of the sort will happen again.'

He stormed off.

'That man must be hell to live with,' I said, watching him go.

'No,' said Cat. 'He's a real softy.'

'He what?'

'He went to very strict schools and he tries to be like his old tutors and seem "in charge". He's not really like that. He has to work at it.'

'If you say so.'

'I do. So stop rubbishing him.'

21

After dinner that night there was organised entertainment. You'll never guess what. A puppet show. Yes, a puppet show, at our age. Miss Piper, the smiliest librarian ever, sat all the kids on chairs in front of a Punch and Judy type booth, except this one wasn't red and white stripes but yellow arrows on black. Highly amusing, I'm sure.

The main puppet characters were a pair of quarrelling convicts called Spike and Joni. Spike set fire to a haystack and Joni stole a pail of milk, and they were arrested, and a judge ordered them to be sent to Scragmoor Jail to 'await your just deserts'. At Scragmoor they were whacked over the head a lot by a turnkey (jailor) and the governor – Mr Battersby – told them they were evil and threatened them with a diet of lumpy porridge and rainwater if they didn't behave. Joni behaved but Spike tried to escape, so he was taken to the executioner, who cackled meanly while he hanged him. It was all done for laughs, with lots of yelling and mad threats, but some in the audience didn't look too entertained.

'Miss,' one of the girls called out, 'we'll have nightmares.'

'Had one already,' muttered one of the boys.

Miss Piper seemed quite taken aback that some of us weren't enjoying the show.

'Oh, that isn't what we want at *all*,' she said. 'We thought it would be a bit of fun, that's all, given our surroundings. Isn't that right, Jack?'

We had no idea Mr Toliver was even in the room until he ducked out from the back of the booth with Spike and the Hangman on his hands. He wasn't in black leathers this time. Mr Toliver, I mean.

'Have we misjudged things, Miss P?' he asked.

'I think we might have,' she said.

Mr Toliver tossed the puppets into the booth. 'Then it's as well that this was just the warm-up for the big event.'

He pushed the booth over to the corner of the room. Only when it was out of the way did we realise that the white wall behind it was a big screen.

'Every Saturday evening will be film night,' Miss Piper told us. 'It's only Thursday now, of course, the first Thursday of your sentence...' – pause for chuckles – 'but we thought we'd show a film anyway. A rather appropriate one, I'm sure you'll agree, after what you've learned about yourselves today.'

She nodded at Jack Toliver and he shouted, 'Ready, Mrs Withering!'

I leaned forward and mouthed 'Mrs Withering?' at Cat, who sat a few seats away from me. She grinned back at me.

The woman who came in pushing a trolley was tall – though not as tall as the Doc, which must have been a relief for her – and she had a friendlier face than him, and less insane hair.

'On Mrs Withering's trolley,' Miss Piper said, 'you'll find popcorn and a selection of ice creams and lollies. Take your pick of one or the other, and when you've made your choice we'll start the film!'

We all collected an ice or little carton of popcorn and returned to our seats. Then the film started and Jack dimmed the lights.

'I've seen this,' someone said when the titles came up.

'Me too,' said someone else.

'Who hasn't?' said Saxon Tull.

It was a superhero movie. Not one of the latest and not one of the greatest. But no one walked out. Better a familiar bunch of unbelievable characters in loopy costumes smacking enemies around than sitting in our cells staring at the walls.

The film was about halfway through when someone cried out. No one paid much attention as we'd got to the standard rooftop chase scene and the music had swelled to match, but when the shout was repeated Jack Toliver, sitting at the side, asked if something was wrong. He must have had some sort of volume control to hand, because the sound went down as he said it.

'Howley's gone!' the shouter replied.

'Howley?'

'Howley Marsh, my cellmate. He was here and now he's not.'

'What are you talking about? I haven't moved.'

'What?' said the first boy.

Jack froze the film and raised the lights. The boy who'd shouted was standing now, staring at the empty seat next to his.

'Howley?' he said.

'Byron, what are you playing at?' said the empty seat.

'Oh, my God,' said Miss Piper, jumping up. 'Howley's invisible!'

Chairs were shoved aside or scrambled over as kids swarmed to get near invisible Howley. 'Stop prodding me!' the empty chair said more than once.

'Do you look invisible to you, Howley?' Miss Piper asked the space he didn't seem to be in.

'I'm not invisible,' he answered. 'Look, there's my hand!'

'We can't see your hand,' Miss said. 'Can't *see* any part of you.'

'Howley,' Mr Toliver said, 'you appear – to use quite the wrong word – to be the fourth student to find your power today!'

'Which must make me the fifth,' said another voice.

The owner of the voice was clinging to the ceiling, with fingers that had turned into suckers.

'I just floated up here and *stuck*!' she said, in a frightened sort of way.

Fortunately for her, when the suckers turned

back into fingers a minute later Jack and a couple of others were there to catch her. Howley Marsh got visible again half a minute later.

The rest of the film was postponed for another time because the only thing most of the kids wanted to do was talk about what their powers might be when they came. I didn't want to get into all that – I'd been trying not to think about the power I seemed to have got – so when Cat jerked her head at me and Speechless, I didn't need a second jerk to get me out of there.

22

We went to the lobby, and out the front door. It wasn't dark yet, but it was getting there.

'So you've got a mother here too,' I said to Cat as we sat down on the steps. 'Did she also adopt you?'

'As well as, not also.'

'And her job is doling out ice cream and popcorn?'

'She's the person you go to when you fall over and scratch your ickle knees,' she said. 'The matron.'

'Doesn't look like he's moved since we left him,' said Speechless.

No need to ask who he meant. Like him, Cat and I looked up.

'Pity there isn't a way to make him stay like that,' I said.

'But there isn't,' said Cat. 'So we have to find his missing eye.'

'I have a better idea.' They turned to me, eager to hear the Big Plan. 'We pretend we never met him and get on with our lives without talking or thinking about him ever again.'

'What about his threat to turn us to stone and put us out on the moor for all eternity?' Speechless asked.

I shrugged. 'Empty words.'

'They didn't sound so empty to me. I hate being out in bad weather, specially for all eternity.'

'I agree,' said Cat. 'We have to try and find that eye.'

'And start where?' I said. 'How do we know it didn't drop out of its socket all the way up there and land all the way down here a century ago?'

'If it did,' said Speechless, 'it would have been swept up or washed away before anyone here was born.'

'Even your dad,' I said to Cat.

'Any of that *might* have happened,' Cat said, 'but as we're here, why don't we look around? If we don't find it, we can eliminate this area from our enquiries.'

So we took a third of the courtyard each, and walked slowly up and down staring at the cobbles and inspecting any greenish stones we came across. None of them turned out to be anything like the gargoyle's existing eye, or even a broken part of it. It soon felt like a pretty silly thing to do, pacing the courtyard staring at the cobbles, and at one point I glanced towards the building hoping no one was watching us, and saw someone step smartly back from one of the windows. Whoever it was they were too quick for me to see who. Could have been anyone, any adult anyway, probably a teacher. The teachers here seemed to be very cheerful and tolerant and so on, but they were still teachers.

'Now what?' Speechless said when we were satisfied the courtyard was gargoyle-eye free.

'Search me,' I said.

'Why, have you got it?'

'It might help,' said Cat, 'if we knew who he was when he was human.'

'I thought you didn't believe he ever was,' I said.

'Yeah, well I've been thinking about that. If a lump of stone shaped like a gargoyle can move and talk and threaten all of a sudden, nothing's impossible.'

'Why would it help knowing who he was?'

'I don't know. But it might.'

'He must have been a prisoner here,' said Speechless.

'He might not have been,' I said. 'Might have been a warder. The warders in some of the photos looked more evil than most of the prisoners.'

'Why would a prison warder be turned into a gargoyle?' Cat said.

'Why would anybody?'

She nodded. 'True.'

'He seems to think a lot of his missing eye,' said Speechless.

'That's because it's not there any more,' Cat said. '"You don't know what you've got till it's gone".' She sang this.

'What's that?' I asked.

'Old song my mother sings sometimes.'

'Your mother sings?'

'In the shower.'

'Did you really have to tell me that?'

'Tell you what?'

'That your mother sings in the shower. Now I'm imagining her.'

'Well please *stop*,' Cat said sternly.

I shuddered. 'Glad to.'

23

When we reached the floor where the bedcells were located Cat went her way (to the girls') and we went ours. In Cell 10, I eyed my mattress on the floor.

'It's not much of a stretch to imagine waking up on that,' I said, 'and finding it isn't the 21st century but the seventeen hundreds and I've been sent here for life for nicking a chicken's egg.'

'Or toys that don't belong to you,' said Speechless.

'Hey, I forgot those.'

I felt in my pocket for the Noah's Ark animals and the wooden marbles. I'd taken them at random, so it was the first time I'd looked at them outside of the display case in the ex-stables. The animals were a lion, a tiger, a giraffe, an elephant and a hippo. There were four marbles. One of them was plain wood, but the others had pictures on them painted by the governor's kids: a green bird, a white flower and a blue one with a bright red flame on it.

'If Spike had taken those he'd have been sent to the Hanging Shed,' Speechless said.

'Spike?'

'The puppet from earlier.'

I went to the bookcase and arranged the animals in a neat row on one of the shelves and wedged the marbles between them to stop them rolling off. As I turned away Speechless went to look at them.

'I had some animals like this once,' he said. 'Not this old, though.' He picked up the elephant and held it up. 'We have an elephant in the room!'

Moving the elephant freed the carefully placed marbles, which rolled to the edge of the shelf. I darted forward, caught three but missed one, which hit the floor and cracked in half.

'Look what you've done!' I said.

'Sorry.'

'Put that elephant back!'

He put it back and said sorry again. The broken marble was the one with the painted white flower.

I tossed its two halves onto Speechless's bunk and returned the other three to my pocket, where they'd be safe.

We didn't say anything else – me out loud or him in my head – while he curled up on his bunk with his book and I hung some things in the wardrobe.

In a while, Marcus Preedy came in. 'Isn't it fantastic?' he said.

'What?' I asked.

'These powers. So exciting. All of it, all this.' He waved an arm around like we were standing by a blue lagoon with palm trees.

'Yeah. Everyone should have a cell like this.'

'I mean the school, what we're here for, might be able to do. And the kids.' He climbed the ladder to the top bunk. 'Specially Saxon.' He swung his legs happily. 'I never met anyone like Saxon. He's so smart, so funny. I really like him, don't you?'

Before I could open my mouth to spit, he carried on, and then it was Saxon this, Saxon that, Saxon the wonderful. I tried to interrupt a few times but it was a lost cause. On and on he went – Saxon, Saxon, Saxon – like a boy possessed. I tried to block him out, but every Saxon got through, until eventually, having heard more about him than seemed reasonable this side of a straitjacket, I said, 'Marcus. Stop. Please.'

I might as well not have spoken. He carried on, and on, and on, shrivelling my ears and shrinking my brain with Saxon Tull worship. So I tried a different approach. I staggered suddenly, clutching my head.

'Oh!' I said. 'I feel a power coming on!'

Now he stopped, jaw frozen somewhere between 'Saxon' and 'Saxon'. Even Speechless turned over and stared.

'Yes,' I said, rolling my eyes. 'I really feel it. It's the power to...wait... Oh! Yes! Got it! The power to explode in tiny pieces and take everyone with me if...' – I paused, then said through gritted teeth – '*if I ever hear the name Saxon Tull in this cell again!*'

My head filled with a whoop of Speechless laughter, but that was the last I heard from Marcus on his new pet subject.

I got down on my mattress, all set for a night's peace and quiet, and maybe the odd sweet dream.

Wishful thinking.

24

I was surrounded by people, dozens of people, shuffling, mournful, all trying not to look at me, like meeting my eye would be the end of them. Then they were gone and I was alone, and it was cold, really cold, and I couldn't move, and the wind howled around me, and I didn't know who I was, or what, or anything at all.

I had a view, though. A very high view across the moor. Not much to look at. Rocks in great heaps, rolling grass, the odd collapsed building, animals dotted about. At first the sky was grey and heavy, but then it broke up, into clouds that flew apart and hurled bolts of lightning at the ground before letting the sun through for a second. Then snow fell, settled, and the moor was completely white for a time, till it dissolved in the blink of an eye, and the moon bounced around the night sky, sometimes full, sometimes not, sometimes just a bright curved—

'Dax! Dax!'

Sharp light. Pain through eyelids.

'Get that thing out of my face!'

Speechless lowered his torch and I tried to blink the negative blobs away.

'You all right?' he asked.

'I was dreaming,' I said.

'No you weren't. Not really.'

'How do you know if I was dreaming or not?'

'I got glimpses. Bouncebacks.'

'Bouncebacks?'

'From you. What you were seeing came from me. But not originally.'

I propped myself up on an elbow.

'Speechless, I just woke up. You just woke me. Either speak a language I understand or shut the hell up.'

'I was getting these images,' he said. 'A view, weather, changing seasons, tormented faces, all flipping by in no particular order.'

'Getting them from where?'

'Not where, who. The gargoyle. It must be him. Who else would see all that, most of it from very high up, over what looked like years and years?'

'All right, so he passed this stuff on to you. Why did

you send it to me?'

He went back to his bunk and sat on the side.

'I didn't mean to. Didn't know I could. It just filled my mind, and sort of spilled out from there.'

'Spilled out to me. Why me?'

He shrugged. ''Cos we're linked, I guess.'

'Linked?' I said. 'Speechless, we're not *linked*.'

'But you can hear me sometimes, pick things up from me.'

'Yes. You have to cut that out. I don't want you in my mind.'

'Dax, what's going on?'

That wasn't Speechless, it was Marcus, peering blearily down from the top bunk.

'Nothing,' I said. 'Nothing at all.'

'You're talking to yourself again. You woke me up.'

'Oh, ever so sorry, please forgive me.'

I threw myself down and rammed my pillow over my head.

25

At breakfast, alone at my personal table, I noticed Speechless talking to Cat at another. She looked fed up. In a minute he came over and sat down.

'Cat picked me up too last night,' he said.

'Picked you up?'

'The stuff I got from the gargoyle. The view, the seasons, the shuffling prisoners. They had to be prisoners, the way they looked.'

'Did she thank you for sharing it with her in the middle of the night?'

'Not exactly. Said I'd better keep out of her head if I wanted mine to stay on my shoulders.'

No one came close to developing any new powers in the first period of the day (Geography with Mr Kanwar) unless you count Sofia Papalia claiming that she suddenly knew, without thinking about it, that there are seventeen countries whose names begin with the letter 'C'. Mr K did a quick check and found nineteen, so Sofia's 'power' was laughed out of the room.

After morning break we were assembled in the courtyard by Ms Samson and Mr Cosmo (in their super costumes, ho-hum).

'We're not going to make a habit of the fancy dress,' Mr Cosmo told us, 'but we thought it appropriate today as we're going to take a stab at enticing super things out of you in the open, among the tors.'

'What are tors?' someone asked.

'The big piles of rock you can't have missed on your way here.'

'What does "tor" mean?'

'Well I *think* the word comes from old Celtic or Gaelic and means something like hill or rocky mound,' Mr Cosmo said. 'That sound about right, Ms Samson?'

'About,' she said.

'Will we have to wear costumes like yours one day?' one girl asked.

Ms Samson smiled. 'Would you want to?'

'Only if I could design my own.'

'No one's putting *me* in tights,' said a boy called Jamal Sarkis.

'And I'm keeping my undies on the *inside*,'

said Howley Marsh.

'It wouldn't matter in your case,' said Saxon Tull. 'You'd be invisible.'

Like most of the unfunny things Tull said this got a round of laughs, and a couple of his disciples raised their hands for the sad palm slap.

'If I had a power,' I said to Cat, 'it would be to throw certain people into orbit.'

'You're quite jealous of him, aren't you?' she said.

'Jealous of Tull? Why would I be jealous of him?'

'Well, because he's popular...friendly...good sense of humour...'

'Good sense of *humour*!'

'And good-looking.'

'Good-*looking*!'

Ms Samson and Mr Cosmo led us across the courtyard, out through the gateless gateposts, onto the road away from Scragmoor. The road to freedom. Cat and I were a few steps behind Ms Samson.

'That woman should *not* wear Lycra,' Cat whispered to me.

She wasn't wrong. Some of Ms Samson's muscles were in places you could do without in pants as tight as hers.

'This should go on YouTube,' I said, whipping my phone out.

'No signal,' said Cat.

'There will be on Saturday.'

I turned it on, but before I could aim it Ms Samson

said, 'Don't you dare,' and turned round.

'How did you know?' I asked.

She grinned. 'Eyes in my bum. It's a super power.'

She turned around, waggled her muscly backside, and continued walking. I laughed. Couldn't help it.

'What are those ruins?' someone asked, pointing way over to the left.

'That was a village in its day,' Mr Cosmo said. 'When the jail was built many of the cottages became the homes of the warders and their families. None of the buildings are usable now—'

'Or safe, so don't go near them,' Ms Samson added.

'Or safe,' Mr Cosmo agreed, 'especially the old chapel, which has just two standing walls left, and only part of its roof intact. But the foundations of most of the buildings are sound, apparently, so they're being adapted for our use as a gym and exercise area.'

'A *reinforced* gym,' Ms Samson said, 'in case any of your powers get a bit too super.'

There was someone standing by the tor we were being led to.

'What's your mum doing here?' I asked Cat.

'Ready and waiting for accidents to happen,' she said.

'Now it could be,' Mr Cosmo said when we were gathered round the tor, 'that the Lomas Gene's potential will be in no hurry to reveal itself in some of you, but it could take us by surprise, as it already has in a few cases. Those who've developed a power already, would you come out front, please?'

Four kids stepped forward. Tilda Riddick, the girl who'd grown suckers and stuck to the ceiling, Tamsin Gorey who turned into furniture, Howley Marsh, who'd become invisible (but wasn't now), and Saxon Tull. Tull took a bow. Well, he would.

'I thought there were five,' said Ms Samson.

'There were,' said Mr Cosmo. He looked around. 'Una? Una Wing?'

'Here.' Una shuffled forward. That girl really didn't like the limelight.

'It'll be interesting to see who gets a power next,' Mr Cosmo said, 'and what it will be.'

'It's not a competition, though,' said Ms Samson. 'No hurry, no pressure.'

'No. Course not. What we'd like you to do is spread

out, climb the rocks, run around, do whatever you fancy within reason. No daft risks, no jumping from high tors, though – and come straight back when you hear my whistle.' He opened a satchel slung over his shoulder. 'Ms Samson and I will be keeping an eye out, but if anything odd happens to any of you give us a shout anyway. Off you go.'

'Even the ones who've already got a power?' Howley Marsh asked.

'Even those,' Mr Cosmo said. 'Who knows? They might develop further.'

'And be careful!' shouted Mrs Withering after the first ones to hare off.

Mr Cosmo took two pairs of binoculars from his satchel and offered one to Ms Samson. 'Up we go, Dot,' he said.

She half reached for the binoculars, but didn't take them. She looked nervous.

'What's wrong?' Mr Cosmo asked her.

'I'm not sure about going up there.'

'But we must. We might not see everything from... Oh. Bothered by heights?'

She nodded. 'High heels make me queasy.'

'I'll go,' said Mrs Withering.

'I don't think so,' Mr Cosmo said. 'What if you fall off? With you out of action there'll be no one to take care of the kids if they need it.'

'Harry, I used to run across rocks all the time as a girl.'

'I'm sure you did, Marie. And that was how long ago?'

She pursed her lips. 'I'm not in a wheelchair *yet*, you know.'

'No, you're not, and we can't afford to have you in one.'

'I could do it,' I said.

Their eyes flipped to me in surprise.

'Don't you want to run around and climb and see if you develop any powers?' Ms Samson asked.

'No. I would just *hate* to get useless muscles.'

I said this because Tull was still there. He scowled, which brought a warm glow to my heart.

'Thanks, Dax,' Mr Cosmo said. He handed me the binoculars. 'But keep your peepers peeled in all directions.'

I looped the strap round my neck. 'You bet.'

26

I hauled myself up onto the first rock, a big round boulder about as high as my shoulder. A shoulder boulder. The rocks were all shapes and sizes and piled onto one another and packed together like a huge puzzle. They were so smooth that it wasn't easy to get a handhold on some of them, or find a way between them, but when I made it to the top – sweating from the climb and glad of the bit of breeze up there – it felt like I'd won something.

'Watchful eye, Dax!' Mr Cosmo shouted. 'Watchful eye!'

He sounded out of breath – not surprising as he'd just climbed the tor next door and wasn't a spring chicken like me. But standing up there, with the light behind him, his blue and red cape fluttering in that bit of breeze, he looked much more heroic than he did on the ground.

I hoisted the binoculars and scanned the moor. Kids running, rolling, jumping, climbing, shouting.

Ponies, sheep and goats tearing at the grass here and there. Ms Samson striding about in her muscle-bound tights. Mrs Withering leaning against a boulder with her face turned up to the sun like she was trying to catch a tan. And above everything the sky as blue as a sky can be, hardly a cloud, a few birds circling the roof of the old jail like vultures looking for bones to pick. Not so bad really.

'Ridley's gone!'

I lowered my binoculars to see who'd said that. Some distance off, one of the boys was looking our way.

'What does "Ridley's gone" mean?!' shouted Mr Cosmo.

'I mean he's vanished! He was here, and now he's not!'

'He's probably hiding! Look around!'

'No, I mean he's disappeared!'

'Ridley?!' Mr Cosmo bawled. 'Ridley, can you hear me?!'

'Yes, sir! They're kidding you! I'm still here!'

'Your voice might be,' someone else said, 'but your body isn't.'

'What do you mean my body isn't? I can see it.'

'Well, I can't.'

'That makes two of us.'

'Three of us!'

'Four!'

'Five!'

'Six!'

'Sounds like a repeat performance of yesterday,' Ms Samson said to Mr Cosmo. 'Howley, was it?'

'Yes,' said Mr Cosmo. 'Is Howley near?'

'Yes!' shouted Howley.

'Are you invisible, Howley?'

Howley stepped forward and waved – not invisibly.

'Ridley, will you wave at us?' Mr Cosmo said.

'I am!' said Ridley.

But no one could see him.

'Well,' said Ms Samson. 'Looks like we have *two* invisible stars now.'

Saxon Tull and his pals jumped down from the tor they'd started to climb and headed off to check out the invisibility of Ridley. Marcus Preedy was one of Tull's followers but he'd climbed faster and higher than the others – probably showing off in front of his hero – so he was still on the tor when they set off. He jumped too now, obviously meaning to go after them, but when his feet left the rock they didn't take him the way gravity usually prefers. They shot out behind him, and next thing he knew...

...he was flying at full stretch towards the school.

I was the only one to see him go. All other eyes were on the place where Ridley wasn't. If Marcus had made some sort of noise they might have looked to see where it came from, but he didn't make a sound. Too shocked, I guess.

But then I heard a voice in my head – 'Hey!' – and saw Speechless gaping after Marcus. Cat heard him too, and also looked, also gaped. She looked my way, stuck her hands out in a 'What the...?' sort of way, and the three of us – me through the binoculars – watched Marcus hurtle through the air like someone fired from a canon, getting higher and higher as he went.

'He's going to hit the school,' Speechless said, loud and clear in my head.

'He's still climbing,' I said, though he couldn't hear me from where he stood. 'Might just clear the roof if he's lucky.'

In fact, from the top of my tor it looked like Marcus would hit the gargoyle. He didn't, though. He was saved by blind terror. Through the binoculars I saw the gargoyle bare his teeth and reach for him like he wanted to grab him, and enfold him, and crush him, and that's when Marcus found his voice and used it to give an ear-crunching scream as he did a somersault that flipped him over and sent him spinning nose over toes, knees over fleas, back the way he'd come.

27

Even if they didn't see him go, everyone heard Marcus's scream as he came back. And when they heard it, all eyes jerked to see where it came from and all mouths gasped when they saw him hurtling towards us. Then there was a lot of shouting and running in wrong directions, like people panicking to get out of the way of a flaming meteorite crashing down through the atmosphere. Marcus was softer than a meteorite, but in half a minute or less he would splat onto one of the tors or the hard ground of the moor itself. Whichever he landed on, the result would be the same as if he'd struck the building.

Lack of survival.

Instant death.

Kaputzville.

But that didn't happen.

Marcus didn't die.

He bounced.

Yes, bounced.

On a trampoline.

A what?

That's right. A trampoline. Which a second earlier hadn't been there.

Marcus bounced and bounced and bounced, then bounced some more, each bounce a bit lower than the last, until he lay spread-eagled on the trampoline, which slowly, gently, sank to the ground, and, moving out from under him, became...

Tamsin Gorey.

'Now that,' said Ms Samson in total awe, 'is what I *call* a power!'

She meant Tamsin, who, amazed as everyone else, said, 'I couldn't help it, it just happened.'

'Help it or not, you saved that boy's life.'

'Sorry, didn't mean to.'

I'd scrambled down from my tor by this time, and so had Mr Cosmo, who was like an excited five year old.

'Tamsin,' he said. 'Yesterday you became a chair when Mr Gladhusband was short of one, and now, when something was urgently needed to prevent Marcus coming to a rather yucky end, you turned into the perfect thing to catch him. A power to become objects when most required? Just a little bit astonishing, that's my verdict.'

'It's much more than merely *astonishing*,' said Mrs Withering. 'Wait till my husband hears about this!'

'And it seems we have our first flyer,' said Ms Samson, leading Marcus to a boulder and sitting him down on it.

'Looked to me like he was *falling*,' said Saxon Tull. He didn't look too happy about someone else being in the limelight.

'Maybe he was,' said Mr Cosmo, 'but he can't have fallen up into the sky in the first place. *Were* you flying, Marcus?'

Marcus looked very dazed. No longer terrified, just dazed.

'I don't know, I just...went.'

'We should get him back to the school,' said Mrs Withering. 'Jack might be able to counsel him through this.'

'Jack plus one other appropriate adult,' said Mr Cosmo.

'Of course.'

When Mrs Withering pulled something out of

her pocket I thought it was a phone at first, but it turned out to be a little walkie-talkie. She spoke into it, then said that she'd alerted Jack and would take Marcus back.

'You don't think you should stay here in case of other accidents?' Ms Samson said.

Mrs Withering looked unsure. 'Well...'

'Which of you is Marcus's cellmate?' asked Mr Cosmo.

'We are,' I said, stepping up beside Speechless.

'Tweedledumb and Tweedledumber,' smirked Saxon Tull.

'Both of you?' said Ms Samson. 'I thought it was two per bedcell.'

'They lost count when they got to us,' I told her.

'Perhaps you should both escort him then. You know where Jack's office is?'

'Yes.'

'Can I go too?' Cat asked.

'I don't think that's necessary, dear,' her mum said.

Cat curled her lip as Speechless and I headed back with Marcus. 'Still wearing the binoculars,' Speechless pointed out as we went.

'I always wanted a pair of binoculars,' I said.

'Like you always wanted someone else's toys?'

'Will you give that a *rest*?' I snarled.

If Marcus had been listening, all he'd have heard would have been my side of this – 'I always wanted a pair of binoculars... Will you give that a rest?' – but he gave no sign of hearing a thing. He didn't say a word all the way back, in fact, and as we crossed the courtyard to the front door he kept his head well down. I looked up, though. Saw the gargoyle leaning right out, craning his neck like he was following our every move with his mean green eye.

Miss Piper was waiting for us at the top of the steps.

'I hear we have a flyer!' she said cheerily.

'Looks like it,' I said. 'We have to take him to Mr Toliver.'

'I know. Jack asked me to sit in with him.'

She reached for Marcus and took him inside, one arm round his shoulders, then walked him gently to Jack Toliver's office. Me and Speechless followed. Marcus didn't say a thing the whole way. Just as we reached a door marked 'Jack's Joint', the door opened.

'No need to ask which of you's the patient,' Jack said. 'What happened exactly?'

'He was shooting through the air,' I explained. 'Must have thought he was going to hit something.'

'What something?'

'The school. Then he sort of panicked and zoomed back in a hurry. Seems to be having trouble getting over it.'

'OK, let's see what we can do about that.'

'Ask him what he's going to do,' Speechless said to me.

I asked Jack what he was going to do.

'Just talk to him really,' he said. 'Talk and listen, help him get whatever it is out of his system. Don't worry, he'll be all right. You can go back to the others now.'

'Ask him how long it'll take,' Speechless said to me.

'Any idea how long it'll take?' I asked.

'Oh, half an hour, tops.'

'I think we should wait,' said Speechless.

'We'll wait,' I said to Jack.

'Right you are. Come on, my lad.'

Then he and Miss Piper led Marcus inside – her

arm still round him – and closed the door, very quietly like it was bedtime, or church.

There were no seats in the corridor, so we walked up and down like we were worried about Marcus, which we weren't because we hardly knew him. We didn't say much while we waited. Nothing *to* say really.

After about twenty-five minutes the door opened again and the three of them came out, smiling. Even Marcus was smiling.

'He's fine now,' Jack said.

'Are you?' I asked Marcus.

'You bet.' He beamed. 'Hey. I can fly!'

'Oh, you're good,' I said to Jack.

He gave me a big white grin. 'I know.'

Miss Piper eyed him when he said that, and he eyed her back, and me and Speechless eyed each other, and nodded. If those two weren't already an item they soon would be.

There didn't seem much point going back to the others now, so Marcus, Speechless and I went outside and sat on the steps.

'So what was it like?' I asked Marcus.

'What was what like?'

'Flying.'

A tiny frown crossed his forehead, but then he smiled again.

'Scary. But kind of cool. I never thought I'd be able to fly. Who could *ever* imagine they'd be able to do that?'

'Want to try again?'

'Again?'

'See if you can take off when you want to.'

'I wouldn't know how.'

'What did you do last time?'

'I don't know, I just sort of...lifted. Then I was away.'

'He might stand more chance of leaving the ground if he's standing on it,' Speechless suggested.

I passed this on to Marcus and we went down the steps.

'Now what?' he asked.

'Well, for starters, how about standing like they do in the comics?'

'I'm not sure how they stand in the comics. My dad doesn't like me reading them.'

I unlooped the binoculars from my neck and handed them to Speechless. He immediately put them to his eyes and looked up at the gargoyle.

'Stand like this,' I told Marcus.

I showed him. Legs apart, torso in a half twist, elbows bent, one arm a little higher than the other, fists clenched, eyes on the sky. He copied me, and there we stood, two idiots trying to look like superheroes all set for liftoff.

'Now concentrate,' I said. 'Think feet leaving ground, think flying.'

'I'll have to close my eyes to think that,' he said.

'OK, close your eyes.'

He closed them. Seconds ticked silently by.

'It's not working,' he said after about half a minute.

'It might not be for you,' I said.

He opened his eyes, and saw what I meant. His feet might not have left the ground, but mine had.

'Heeeeey!' said Speechless, lowering the binoculars and also noticing.

But then Marcus's feet also parted company with the cobbles, and there we were, hovering, the two of us, still in our fists-raised dumbo-hero poses.

But not for long.

Marcus was off – up, up and away – while I slumped back to the ground.

'Tell him to be careful,' Speechless said.

'Be careful!' I shouted.

He didn't go far. About two floors, that's all, then he wobbled, spread his arms to steady himself, and started to come slowly down, feet first. He was about two metres above the ground when the other kids, with the three adults, streamed through the gateless gateposts. A whoop went up when they saw Marcus hovering, which threw him off balance, so that he dropped the rest of the way harder than he probably wanted to. He wasn't hurt, though, and didn't seem to mind everyone thronging round him, asking questions. Mr Cosmo noticed that Speechless had his binoculars and took them back. Cat asked us how it had gone with Jack.

'He's a genius,' I said. 'If I ever have a problem I'll know where to go. Any more powers occur out there?'

'A third invisible case. Jamal. Maybe invisibility's a boy thing. Fine with me. The more boys that go invisible the happier I'll be.'

'No one's forcing you to hang around with us,' I said.

'I know. It's your irresistible charm.'

'Dax nearly got a second power a minute ago,' Speechless told her.

'A *second* power?' Cat said. 'He can't have a second power. Didn't you hear my dad say that the Gene only allows one?'

'I can't help that. Dax's feet left the ground.'

'Oh yes? What did he do – jump?'

'He almost flew.'

'*Almost* flew? Anyone can *almost* fly.' She fluttered her arms. 'Look at me, almost flying.'

'Do it again,' Speechless said to me. 'Show her.'

'No.'

I jogged up the steps and indoors.

Later, though, I slipped away to the North Wing. Perfect place for secret flying, the North Wing. No ceilings to stop you shooting to the clouds, and no spectators. I took the same pose as before, legs apart, torso in a half twist, elbows bent, one arm a little higher than the other, fists clenched, and willed myself to fly.

And willed.

And willed.

And willed.

The only part of me that left the ground was my heels, and that was because I stood on tiptoe.

28

I would have been happy to never talk about the gargoyle's lost eye again, or where it might have got to, but Cat seemed to want to talk about nothing else. She kept on and on about it until I gave in just to shut her up.

'All right,' I said, 'all right, all right, where next?'

'The underground museum complex.'

'Why there?'

'Because nothing's been touched down there since it was the main part of the museum.'

'Why would the eye be in a museum?'

'It probably wouldn't be. But my dad says the museum people made very few changes to the lower floors when they took over, so it's much like it was there when Scragmoor was a prison. And as the gargoyle must have been on the roof during those days, it seems likely that he lost his eye then. Now are there any more questions or can we get started?'

The lower floors were reached through a little side door in the Infirmary. You descended step by step into a whole other world. A world that smelt of age and dust and misery. There were three floors, going down and down, which meant no windows. There were light bulbs here and there, dim ones, tucked well away, which helped the atmosphere if atmosphere was what you wanted. We didn't. We were looking for an eyeball.

Like Cat said, everything looked like it hadn't been touched for ages, and it was spooky quiet. There were corridors and alcoves and half-open cupboards with cobwebs and fake rats and spiders, and drawings and photos on the walls of people who'd been sent to the jail for unforgivable crimes like stealing a loaf of bread to feed a starving child. There were loads of cells, really mean and miserable cells, with heavy black doors or floor-to-ceiling bars that even the scrawniest and smallest prisoners couldn't have squeezed through. There were life-size waxworks in many of them, standing or crouching or lying hopelessly on thin mattresses or beds of straw. A lot of them were kids. None of the model prisoners looked too thrilled to be there. In fact, in those surroundings and that gloom, they looked like unhappy ghosts.

We didn't say much while we poked around down there, and when we did we whispered it. You had to whisper somehow. Even Speechless, talking into our heads, sounded like he was whispering.

'We'll never find an eyeball down here,' I said after we'd been there longer than any of us liked. 'It could be in some cobwebby corner, under the straw in one of the cells, down a crack in the floor, anywhere at all. And we can't even *get* to everything with so many of the doors locked.'

Cat nodded. 'We need a clue.'

'How do we get one of those?'

'We ask the gargoyle if he's remembered anything else.'

'You mean go and see him again?'

'Well, no, I thought we'd shout up to him from the courtyard. Of course go and see him again.'

'You don't mean tonight?' Speechless said with pretty obvious dismay.

'Nah. The morning'll do.'

'We have lessons in the morning,' I said.

'We'll go before lessons.'

'There's not much time between breakfast and lessons.'

'I mean before breakfast. Seven o'clock.'

'Seven? That's almost the middle of the night.'

'It's agreed then,' Cat said. 'The stairwell, 7 A.M. And don't be late.'

29

I would have been late if I'd been allowed, but Speechless had a little alarm clock and he set it, the swine. I didn't hear it go off, but he kicked my feet until one of them woke up, followed by the rest of me. Marcus slept through the alarm. Probably sweet-dreaming about flying with his hero, Tull.

We got to the stairwell at seven-five exactly. Cat wasn't there. She turned up at 7.15.

'You said don't be late,' I reminded her.

'I said that because I expected you to be,' she said.

We climbed over the UNSAFE ENTRY FORBIDDEN sign and started up, her eyes lighting the way ahead, Speechless's little torch lighting my behind.

When we got to the platform at the top I was brought forward to climb the ladder and slide the bolt back. I eased the trap down and clambered out onto the roof. I shivered. This high up, this early, it was a bit breezy there.

The gargoyle turned round as the others

climbed out.

'Back so soon?' he said. 'You have it already?'

'Wish we had,' I said, 'but we've looked everywhere.'

'Not *everywhere*,' said Speechless.

'Everywhere we could think of. We came back because we're stuck.'

'We were wondering if you might be able to sort of...direct us,' said Cat.

'Direct you? I told you, I don't know where my lovely eye went.'

'Yeah, but we hoped you'd have got some more memories back and could give us something to go on that you couldn't before.'

'Well, since you ask,' the gargoyle said, 'I have recalled a few things.'

'Oh yeah? Like...?'

'Men in uniform.'

'Men in uniform?'

'And cells full of wailing, crying, shouting, unchristian language – lots of unchristian language, quite shameful – and a man with very impressive muttonchops.'

'Muttonchops?' I said.

'Big side-whiskers,' said Speechless.

'And a rope,' the gargoyle said. 'I could almost *feel* the texture of that rope.'

He moved his head about, like he was feeling the rope round his neck and enjoying it. Then he stretched his wings, and his single eye glinted.

'Oh, the power. It grows inside me. Grows and spreads. The way I'm going I should soon be able to fly off this roof and get back to what I do best.'

'Which is what?' I asked.

He turned his eye on me. 'Life-taking.'

'Oh. That.'

'But before I return to my humble trade I must have my eye back. I won't feel complete without it. I so want to be complete.'

'We get that,' said Cat. 'So if you can manage to dig something useful out of your memory to help us find it...'

'A few names maybe,' said Speechless.

'Names?'

'As a starting point. Like, say, the moniker of the man with the muttonchops.'

The gargoyle seemed to give this a bit of thought,

and then his lids fell like shutters over his eye and the unoccupied socket next door, and once they were down he didn't move for so long that we looked at one another in a 'Has-he-drifted-off?' sort of way.

He hadn't drifted off. He'd been trying to feel his way into his memory. And he succeeded, a bit. Without raising his eyelids, he recited four names.

'Edrik Gawkson...Mantris Bone...Peter Bittern... Joseph Morgan...'

'Anyone got a pen?' said Cat.

'No need,' said Speechless, tapping the side of his head.

'You'll forget them.'

'I won't. I have a very good memory.'

'Prove it.'

'Edrik Gawkson, Mantris Bone, Peter Bittern, Joseph Morgan. Haven't you realised yet? I'm brilliant.'

'And Little Jamie,' said the gargoyle, uncovering his eye and socket.

'Who's Little Jamie?' I asked.

'I can't remember.'

'Who are any of them?' asked Cat.

'You asked for names, and now you have some,' the gargoyle said. 'You want me to do your job for you?'

'Yes please,' said Speechless.

'You know, I've been thinking about my threat to turn you three to stone,' the gargoyle said then.

'Yeah, so have we,' said Cat. 'Bit extreme, we thought.'

'Extreme? No, far from it, quite the reverse.'

'How'd you mean?'

'I mean why stop at three? There are a lot of people in the building below. No, don't deny it. I can't see them, can't hear them, but I can sense them.'

'What about them?'

'I've decided that if my magnificent eye isn't back in place by the designated hour, they too will be turned to stone.'

'That wouldn't be very fair,' Cat said. 'They haven't done anything.'

'Neither have you.'

'We have. We've searched high and low –'

'Low anyway,' I said.

' – and haven't managed to come up with anything yet, that's all.'

'Then I suggest you try harder,' the gargoyle said, 'because here's the new plan. If you fail me I shall expand my displeasure to include everyone below this roof. Unlike you three, however – you *fortunate* three – they will not enjoy the passing of a thousand seasons and countless sunsets and risings of the moon, but be heaped one upon the other, to turn slowly into tors, adding substantially to the total of lives cut short by the life-taker of Scragmoor.'

He thrust his great bony skull forward, so that it was just a gargoyle breath away, and stared at us with his gleaming green eye. His lips reared back, and he showed a dozen of the sharpest, stoniest teeth you ever had nightmares about, and added, in a voice like oiled thunder:

'*Do I make myself clear?*'

And you know, the last place we suddenly wanted to be was on that roof. We backed away, fast. Two of us did anyway. The one who didn't back away, fast or slow, was me. I wanted to. I mean I *really* wanted to. But I was rooted to the spot. To the roof. Not with terror, though. As I stood there, facing the gargoyle, something dark and mean drove up like a fist from my guts to my chest to my head, and my arms lifted sideways and my fingers went all fluttery, and I felt myself grow taller and broader, and my mouth began to move around, side to side and up and down, like it was trying to get used to having more teeth than usual, and I heard a deep, fierce growl – from my own throat.

The gargoyle's eye widened in what looked like shock. 'What...are you?' he asked.

'Me?' I said. 'What do you mean what...?'

I stopped, because my voice was like his. Deep, gravelly, dangerous.

But then my fingers stopped fluttering, and I lost all that extra size, and my mouth felt like it had the normal quantity of teeth again, and the gargoyle's expression changed to something like I'm-gonna-rip-your-lungs-out-and-feed-them-to-the-crows fury.

'*Are you mocking me, boy?*' he said in his fiercest voice yet.

'Who, me?' I said, in a much higher pitch than before. 'No, no, I just...' I gulped. 'Look, tell you what, why don't I...you know...leave?'

My feet didn't need a lot of encouragement this time. They flipped around and practically skidded me to the hole in the roof, where Cat and Speechless stood with mouths almost as wide as the hole itself, if not so square. I dived head first into the hole and down the ladder hand over hand, knees bumping after me, rung by rung.

Speechless was next down, leaving Cat to come last.

'What *was* that?' Speechless asked while Cat bolted the trap, illuminating the platform with her green glow.

'What did you see?' I asked.

'We saw you half turn into a gargoyle just like him up there,' Cat said.

'I turned into a *gargoyle*?'

'Half turned. You were getting there. You got a lot bigger, some muscles, and wings.'

'I had *wings*?'

'For a second. It looks like your Lomas Gene needs to decide what power to give you.'

'Let's hope it sticks with that one,' said Speechless.

'That one?' I said. 'You *want* me to turn into a gargoyle?'

'Yeah. Then you could start a little club. Just two members, meeting on the roof once a week to talk about missing eyes and stuff, letting Cat and me off the hook.'

We had to wait till lunchtime to talk about what to do next. Then we grabbed a snack and went outside, sat on the steps.

'The names the gargoyle gave us,' Speechless said. 'Maybe one of those people stole his eye.'

'We don't know anyone stole it,' I said.

'No, but if someone did and it was one of them, maybe knowing which one would give us a clue where he put it.'

'We could look through the Scragmoor books in the library,' Cat said. 'See if some of the names are mentioned.'

'They might be mentioned in the old stables too,' I said.

'Old stables?'

'There's some stuff there with names attached.'

'Also in the Hanging Shed,' said Speechless.

'All right,' Cat said. 'Dax, you go to the stables, Speechless to the Hanging Shed, I'll do the library.'

'I'm not going to the Hanging Shed on my own,' said Speechless.

'And don't look at me,' I said, when she did.

'Wimps,' said Cat.

'OK, you do the Hanging Shed.'

'No. I'm doing the library. You two do what you like. But write those names down for me first,' she told Speechless.

He wrote the names down and Cat went her way and we went ours – to the ex-stables, both of us. There, Speechless went to the big glass display cabinet and I headed for the third stall along and the information board on the wall.

'Hey, have you seen this old skull?' he said.

'Yes. Probably a prisoner's. A dead one. We're here to look for names, not admire skulls.'

'There's nothing to say who it belonged to.'

'It doesn't *matter* who it belonged to. What were they again?'

'What were what?'

'The names.'

'Edrik Gawkson, Mantris Bone, Peter Bittern, Joseph Morgan, Little Jamie.'

'I've found Joseph Morgan and Peter Bittern,' I said.

'Really? Already?'

He came over and stood with me, reading the info on the board. Peter Bittern was the hangman whose dad had the job before him. Joseph Morgan was a prisoner. There wasn't a picture of him, but there was a note.

In June 1898 Joseph Morgan, a farmhand, was arrested for the murder of dairy maid Enid Manners, whose body was found on Scrag Moor. Found guilty of the crime, Morgan was hanged at the jail that September. Around 12,000 people (including children) turned out to witness his final moments. Enid's ghost is still said to appear at Flat Tor on the anniversary of her death.

'There's another one,' Speechless said, tapping the board.

The other one was Edrik Gawkson, also a prisoner. He was hanged for breaking into a shop. The note by his name didn't say who the hangman was, but if everyone on the gargoyle's list except Peter Bittern was a prisoner the odds were that he hanged all four. I mentioned this to Speechless. He agreed that it was a fair bet.

'And we have a date now too,' he said.

'A date?'

'1898. The year Joseph Morgan was here. If the gargoyle knew him, it must have been that year, which could also be when his eye disappeared.'

'You think Morgan stole it?'

'Morgan, Gawkson, Bittern, or one of the two we haven't found yet.'

'Look at him,' I said.

A man was glaring at me from a photo of him and several others. The others didn't look too friendly either, but he was the only really short one. The caption didn't say much, just that this was a group of convicts, like we wouldn't have guessed from the matching outfits and chains round their ankles.

I tapped the very short man. 'Little Jamie?'

'Little Jamie might have been a jokey nickname,' said Speechless. 'Like "Little John" in Robin Hood. Little John was the tallest outlaw in the forest.'

'Yeah, but I have a feeling about this one.'

'OK, let's say this is Little Jamie, which leaves just one to find. Oh, look. There was a riot here once.'

'A riot?'

He pointed to a photocopy from an old newspaper article. In 1895, it said, a bunch of prisoners tore up some iron railings and smashed chunks of stone out of walls. They hauled the chunks up to the roof and started lobbing them at the warders in the courtyard below. They didn't lob that many, though, because the warders loaded their muskets and fired, and two of the rioters were killed and the rest gave up and came down.

'Those bits of stone on the roof must be what they left behind,' he said.

'Yeah. Let's go and tell Cat about the names.'

Just before we left, Speechless went back to the display cabinet and stuck his hand in the gap I'd made on my last visit. His hand was smaller than mine, so he got further than I did.

'What are you doing?' I asked.

'Touching the skull.'

'What for?'

'Luck.'

'Since when is touching the skulls of dead jailbirds lucky?'

'I don't know if it is, but it might be.'

I was about to turn away when a photo in the cabinet caught my eye. The one I'd noticed last time, of Governor Hext and his three kids. I pointed the governor out to Speechless.

'Would you call all that cheek fungus muttonchops?'

'Definitely. You think that's the man the gargoyle meant?'

'Has to be. Look at the dates. He was governor from 1887 to 1903 – while Joe Morgan was here.'

'I wonder if his kids miss their toys?' Speechless said.

'Toys?'

'The Noah's Ark animals and marbles that some criminal took. Some really terrible person who deserves to be taken out and hanged.'

'Let's go and find Cat,' I said.

We went to the library, but Cat wasn't there. Miss Piper said she had been and she'd taken some books to the TV lounge.

There were a few kids in the lounge, but the TV screen was blank. No DVDs during the day. Cat was curled up in an armchair reading one of the books. Others were piled in the chair next to her.

'Our gargoyle wasn't the original,' she said as we joined her.

'Original what?' I asked.

She held up the spread she'd been looking at, which showed a drawing of a gargoyle. Just as ugly and horrible as the one we knew, but not him.

'According to this, the first gargoyle was Scragmoor's architect and builder, a man named Thomas Madder.'

I laughed. 'They made a statue of him looking like *that*?'

'No statue. The story goes that Madder was so proud of his building that he took up residence on the roof so he could watch the new prisoners being brought in down below, and count them, but one stormy night he was struck by lightning, and' – she looked up – 'turned into a gargoyle.'

I smirked. 'If you believe that you'll believe anything.'

'I'm just telling you what it says here, not that I believe it – necessarily.'

'Does it say how that gargoyle got replaced by another?' Speechless asked.

'I haven't looked at the other books yet,' Cat said, 'but there's nothing here about a second gargoyle. There is a mention of an old legend, though...'

'Legend?'

'That someone who's been turned into a gargoyle can regain his human form if a stone-hearted person touches him. Then the toucher becomes a gargoyle instead. So maybe an evil man – a serial killer, for instance – got onto the roof, laid hands on the Madder gargoyle, and grew stone wings for his pains.'

'Yes,' I said, 'and maybe it's all a bunch of hooey. You were supposed to be looking for names, not reading fairy tales.'

'I found three straight off,' Cat said. 'Two of them belonged to prisoners, the other to a hangman.'

'Was the hangman Peter Bittern?' Speechless asked.

This took her by surprise. 'How'd you know that?'

'Because we found him too. There was a picture of him. He didn't look like someone you'd want to spend a heap of time with.'

'The two prisoners I found *didn't* spend a heap of time with him. He hanged them. I'm only *guessing* it was him who hanged them, but as his name's on the same list, and he was a hangman, it seems likely.'

'The hanged prisoners. Were they Edrik Gawkson and Joseph Morgan?'

She looked at the list. 'I have Joseph Morgan and Mantris Bone.'

'We found Morgan and Gawkson,' I said. 'Bone completes the set.'

'The set? You found Little Jamie too?'

'A picture that seemed to fit.'

'How could a picture fit a name?'

'He was very short.'

'A lot of people are short. Look at Speechless.'

'Speechless wasn't a convict at Scragmoor Jail. We

also found Muttonchop Man. He was the governor at the time the men on the list were here.'

'And we've pinpointed a year,' said Speechless. '1898. Joseph Morgan was only here that year.'

'You think that's when the gargoyle lost his eye?'

'That or the year he *became* a gargoyle.'

'People who are hanged don't usually turn into gargoyles.'

'Maybe he was an especially bad man.'

'All right,' I said, 'so we've identified the owners of the five names and the man with the muttonchops. And our next step is...?'

'To pay the gargoyle another visit,' Cat said.

'Another one? So soon? I don't know why we don't just move up there.'

'We have to tell him what we've found out about the people attached to the names he gave us and see if any of the info jogs something. What else can we do with nothing else to go on and time running out?'

At the end of lessons she said she some stuff to do but would be in the lobby at four, where she would expect to find me and Speechless waiting for her.

I looked in the crowd of kids swarming out of their classrooms but Speechless had already skedaddled. I eventually found him in our bedcell, lying on his bunk, reading.

'I've been looking for you,' I told him.

'Well, you found me,' he said.

'We're supposed to be meeting Cat in the lobby. Latest trip to the roof, remember?'

'I know, but I wanted a bit of solo time to go through the books from the library.' He got off his bunk and held up the book he'd been looking at. 'Dax, I might have found something. About the gargoyle.'

'Great. Tell us on the way to see him.'

'No, hold on, you'll want to hear this.'

'It can wait. Come on.'

'All right, but...'

He tore a page out of the book.

'Another hanging offence,' I said.

He folded the page into a pocket and we went down to the lobby. Cat looked at her watch as we approached.

'Don't start,' I warned her.

We went to the stairwell, hung around checking one another's fingernails until the last person in the vicinity wandered off, and climbed over the UNSAFE ENTRY FORBIDDEN sign.

'This is starting to feel like a bad habit,' I said.

'Stop whining,' said Cat.

On the way up I told her that Speechless thought he'd got something on the gargoyle. She asked him if it was anything we could use.

'Oh, I'm not sure if we can use it,' he said. 'But it's interesting.'

'We don't need interesting, we need useful,' Cat said.

'It *might* be that too. It depends on a couple of things.'

'Well save it till it is.'

'Yes, but—'

'I said save it,' she snapped.

'You've been living with the Doc too long,' I said.

'He hates being called Doc,' she answered.

'I know, that's why I do it. Is there anything you hate being called?'

'Yes. Tolerant with boys.'

32

At the top of the stairwell I did my thing and climbed out first. The gargoyle was in his usual position, leaning out from the edge of the roof, as still as the statue he was supposed to be.

'Wakey-wakey, Mr Gargoyle,' I said.

One of his wings jumped, like I'd startled him. He turned to look at us, but it was me that his eye – his single eye – seemed to want to be glued to.

'Should I be afraid of you?' he growled suspiciously.

I would like to have said, 'Yes, be afraid, be very afraid,' but what came out was, 'Afraid of me? Hey, no, sorry about earlier, what do you say we forget that ever happened?'

'You must have considerable power to change yourself like that,' he said.

'What?' I said. 'No. You're the powerful one. I reckon it's the power in you that changed me.'

'The power in me...' He thought this over, then nodded slowly. 'It's true that I'm getting more powerful by the hour.'

'Powerful enough to have got some new memories since our last chat?' Cat asked.

'Well, I've remembered some more names.'

'Names. Hmm. Not sure more names will help much. Might just make things more complicated than they need to be.'

'I believe they were the names of condemned prisoners,' the gargoyle said, like she hadn't spoken.

'Maybe they came back to you because you were one of them,' I suggested.

His eye widened. 'You think I was one of the condemned?'

'You must have been. You called yourself a life-taker. Why else would you have been in jail?'

He gave what sounded kind of like a chuckle. But only kind of. The kind that sends rats scurrying down your spine and makes your tongue stick to the roof of your mouth.

'I wasn't *in* jail,' he said. 'The lives I took were *of* the condemned. I was the executioner!'

Cat and I stared at him. Then at each other. Then at Speechless. Speechless was the only one who didn't seem surprised.

'That's what I was trying to tell you,' he said. 'Part of it anyway.'

I turned back to the gargoyle. 'So you were Peter Bittern,' I said.

'Pardon me?'

'The executioner at the time the other people whose names you gave us were here. His dad was hangman before him.'

'He was?' said Cat.

'Yeah, didn't we say?'

'No. You didn't.'

'I wasn't Peter Bittern,' said the gargoyle.

'Of course you were,' I said.

'No, no. He was the hangman before *me*. I recalled that a little while ago. Bittern's surly manner upset the governor's children and led to his dismissal. The children liked me, however. I made them laugh.'

'Laugh?' I said. '*You* made them *laugh*?'

'So what was your name?' Cat asked the gargoyle.

He shook his head. 'I do not yet have that information.'

'I can tell you who you were,' said Speechless.

Three heads swung his way. He took out the page from the library book and stepped forward unfolding it, then held it up for the gargoyle to see. Just the gargoyle, not Cat and me.

The gargoyle flinched at what he saw.

'I was *him*?'

'If you were the one who took over from Peter Bittern when he got the push in 1898,' Speechless said. 'Recognise him?'

'I'm...not sure.'

'Well, it was a while ago.'

'Why is he holding his hand over his eye?'

'I don't know, I wasn't there.'

'Let's see,' said Cat.

Speechless turned the paper round and showed us the picture.

'I've seen that face before,' I said.

'In the ex-stables,' said Speechless. 'He was on the board with some of the other hangmen, including Peter and Edward Bittern.'

'Right, yes. He was winking in that one.'

'Yes. Winking in that one, covering the winked eye in this.'

'Why would he hide his eye?' Cat asked.

'I didn't like it to appear in photographs,' the gargoyle said.

We turned back to him in surprise.

'You remember that but not your name?' I said.

'Yes. I didn't earlier, but I do now. That eye was very personal to me. I didn't like it to be recorded for just anyone to see.'

'Oh!' said Speechless. 'It was a *false* eye.'

'False?' The gargoyle scowled. 'It was the truest eye one man ever created for another.'

'You mean...' said Cat hesitantly.

'He wasn't born with it,' said Speechless.

'What a pity we didn't know that before,' I said.

'It wouldn't have made any difference. We still wouldn't have had a clue where to look for it.'

Cat took the page and studied the photo.

'Quite a smile he's got there,' she said.

'Yes,' Speechless said. 'He might have lost his eye, but he never lost the smile.'

'How do you know that?'

'It said so on the page I didn't tear out. He was born with his mouth turned way up at the corners, and it stayed that way, even when he was in a stinking mood. No wonder he was nicknamed Smiler Spewdrift.'

'Spewdrift?' said the gargoyle.

'Collymore Spewdrift,' Speechless said.

'Collymore Spewdrift. That sounds...familiar.'

'He was a rope maker by profession. He made the ropes for Scragmoor's executioners. Lived with his wife in a cottage on the moor. In August 1898, after Peter Bittern got the chop, the governor called him in to handle the hangings.'

'And you couldn't have told us this before?' I said to him.

'I tried. You didn't want to know. Either of you.'

The gargoyle was staring at the ground between him and us. 'I want you to go now,' he said.

'But you haven't given us anything we can use,' said Cat. 'If you still want us to find your eye – your non-biological eye – we need something new to go on. Unless you don't want it back now...?'

The gargoyle lifted his head. 'I do. More than ever. Go!'

Cat went to the trapdoor hole and dropped down it, and Speechless followed her. I'd just swung my legs over the side when the gargoyle spoke again.

'Little Jamie,' he said. It was almost a whisper.

'What?'

'Little Jamie took my beloved eye.'

'You just remembered that?' I said.

'I did.'

'Coming thick and fast now, aren't they? Maybe we should stick around in case you get something that's actually helpful.'

'No. Go. Find it, and quickly, or feel my wrath.'

'That's still on then, is it?' I said. 'The turning us to stone plan, putting us out on the moor for all eternity, piling everyone else up to become tors?'

'It is,' he said in his deepest, darkest, growliest voice. 'And time, like my patience, is fast running out.'

He turned away, leaned out over the edge of the roof, and ceased to move.

The next day was Saturday. No lessons, no regrets. When we went down we found Mrs Withering surrounded by a swarm of kids in the entrance hall. They seemed excited about something and she was trying to calm them down.

'I *imagined* that you were told about it at the outset,' she was saying.

'We weren't,' said one boy.

'It's true then, is it, Miss?' a girl asked.

'It's not my place to discuss it. I would if I could, but... Ah, Mr Gladhusband, just the man!'

The kids swarmed from her to Mr Gladhusband and started badgering him instead, but they got just as little out of him. I saw Cat standing a bit away from all this. There was a secretive sort of smile on her face.

I went to her and asked what was going on.

'There's a rumour going round,' she said.

'About?'

'SH1.'

'What's that?'

'I can't say.'

'You mean you don't know?'

'I mean I can't say.' She zipped her lips to prove it.

In the Infirmary we heard that two girls had developed a power overnight. One of them – Lisa something – could suddenly make her arms grow very long, which turned out to be handy for serving herself before others at breakfast. The other girl, Amalia Damonte, could make objects burst into flame by wriggling a finger at them. She demonstrated this by pointing at a table and setting off the fire alarms. After that, everyone kept well away from her.

One boy found that the power he'd already got had developed a bit. Saxon Tull. He strode into the Infirmary with bulgy muscles and an even bulgier grin, and picked up two boys by an arm apiece and held them off the ground. One of the boys thought this was a hoot, but the other yelled to be put down, which made Tull laugh and hold him even higher.

'Oh, why couldn't *he* have got invisibility?' I groaned.

Tull must have caught this, or my expression,

because he shouted across at me. 'Hey, Daley, gonna show us what *you* can do?'

He made to chuck the nervous boy at me. He didn't let go of him, just wanted to see me duck. He got his wish.

After breakfast there was a scrum around the room called the Com Centre, which was open for the first time and packed with kids using various devices to chat, text, tweet and so on, like they hadn't been in touch with the world for months. There were two things we'd all been asked not to talk about to anyone outside the school. One was the Lomas Gene and the powers it was expected to give us. The other was Scragmoor Prime being anything other than what Mr Soldoni called 'a normal educational establishment'.

'It's bound to get out, all that,' I said to Cat and Speechless. 'And when it does, the place'll be surrounded by journos, photographers and TV crews.'

'I don't think it will,' said Cat.

'Course it will. They'll be here by the Jeepload, hovering in helicopters, banging on the door demanding the full story, with pictures, interviews, the works.'

She shook her head. 'Things have been put in place.'

'What things?'

Once again she wouldn't say any more, but I got the idea when I took a turn in the Com Centre and phoned my folks.

'Hi, Mum.'

'Dax! Great to hear from you!'

'Yeah, must be. Having a quiet time there without me?'

'We miss you, darling.'

'And I miss my room, my things, my friends, everything I've been deprived of. You really dumped on me, didn't you?'

'Aren't you enjoying it there?' she asked.

'Enjoying it? I'm not even meant to *be* here.'

'Not meant to be there? You are. You were selected.'

'Yes. About that. It was a mistake. I—'

Suddenly there was a weird humming on the line. A humming that stopped when Mum said: 'Sorry, Dax, didn't catch that.'

I started again. 'There was some sort of administrative error. It's this Gene thi—'

The humming again, blocking out the rest.

Puzzled, I saw Cat watching me.

'Get it now?' she said.

I tried again, with Dad this time, and again the humming started when I tried to tell him anything worth saying. The call didn't last long after that. As I clicked off I heard a girl near me say the text she'd written had broken up.

'Were you writing about what we do here, or the Gene?' asked Mr Gladhusband, who'd looked in to see how everyone was getting on.

'No.' But her guilty look told a different story.

'Because if you were, I suggest you find another subject.'

I asked the girl what happened. She showed me her text. It looked fine until she started to say something about the Gene. Then the words became random letters and symbols. She said the message hadn't changed while she was writing it, only when she was about to send it.

'So anything about the Gene or Scragmoor is chopped?' I said to Cat.

'So I'm told.'

'Who by? The old buzzard?'

'Let's go outside.'

34

Over breakfast Miss Niffenegger had told us that we were to assemble in the courtyard at ten for a special announcement from the Head. Most of the students were already there by the time we went out. Some were just chatting, others were jumping about, hoping to encourage their Gene to give them the power they couldn't wait to have.

Two boys had got a power since breakfast. One was Rendell Bude, whose power was running super fast. He was showing it off by dashing from one side of the courtyard to the other in two seconds flat, then doing the same thing in another direction. People were keeping their heads down all over the yard in case he zoomed their way.

The other boy, Byron Flood, claimed to have got super hearing. When he paid attention, Byron said, he could hear the grass moving out on the moor.

'Why would you want to hear grass?' Damian Lee asked him.

'I don't, I'm just saying.'

'Can you hear the rocks too?'

'Rocks don't make any noise.'

'How about clouds?'

'Or them. But I can hear you, and I wish you'd stuff a cork in your mouth, or better still tape it up.'

'Maybe we should use sign language when talking about the you-know-who and the you-know-what in case Byron picks us up,' Cat said.

'I don't speak sign language,' I said.

'I can say as much as I like without it,' said Speechless.

'You'd better do all the talking for the three of us then,' said Cat.

'Wa-heeeey!'

That came from about three floors up, where the girl whose fingers had turned to suckers in the TV lounge, clung to the wall with one hand while waving to the rest of the world with the other.

'Tilda!' This was Miss Piper, running down the steps. 'Do you need reminding what happened last time you clung to something high up?'

'Yes, Miss, but the suckers seem to have more grip this time.'

'They might have more grip, but it might be just as temporary. My advice is to experiment with duration nearer the ground before you climb that high.'

Tilda climbed down the side of the building with both suckered hands. She was about five feet from the ground when the suckers turned back into fingers, but it gave Miss Piper a chance to say, 'See?' as she helped her to her feet.

Some of the kids were talking to a couple of tutors, asking questions and so on. One of the questions I overheard was George Bergoglio asking Mrs Page-Turner why a few kids had got a power already but not all. She said that no one knew, but that George must be patient and he'd probably get his before long. The words were hardly out of her mouth when he grew to twice his normal height and turned yellow, and his breath became a cloud of ice that crashed to the ground and shattered.

Mrs Page-Turner laughed and clapped her hands. 'I have the power of prophecy!'

Another question was Una Wing's. She asked Mr Gladhusband how she could control her power to make things levitate. 'When I try to make it work it doesn't,' she said, 'and twice yesterday I made things lift into the air without meaning to.'

'One of them was me,' said Elinor Ruffgarden. 'I wasn't best pleased.'

Mr Gladhusband told Una that we were all new to this, that no one knew anything, that it was going to be trial and error all the way. 'If it's getting you down,' he said to her, 'why not go and see Jack Toliver? It's his job to help you all through any concerns you might have. I hear he's rather good at it too.'

When Dr Withering came out, his wife was with him. He stopped halfway down the steps, but she carried on to the bottom and stood there looking around until everyone stopped talking and messing about and turned to face the Doc.

'Morning, students!' he said heartily. 'I've called you here this morning because it's come to my notice that a rumour has begun to circulate about the precise function of Scragmoor Prime. I would have come to this before long anyway, but, as I always do as I'm told by certain individuals' – he glared in a not-too-serious way at his wife at the foot of the steps – 'I'm going to spill the beans now. It won't take long, and then you're free to enjoy your weekend in virtually any way you see fit – we plan a hike across the moors tomorrow afternoon, by the way, if the weather remains clement...'

'Does he take so long to get round to *everything*?' I whispered to Cat.

'You should hear him talk about the best way to butter toast,' she said.

Mrs Withering must have thought the same as me because she said, 'Horace. Please. It'll be dark before you're done at this rate.'

'Scragmoor Prime,' the Doc went on, 'is a free school in the sense that while we're obliged to teach the essential academic subjects, we're allowed to pursue a range of specialised ones, the like of which has already been explained to you. Scragmoor is unlike other free schools, however, in that it is funded by a specially set up government department called SH1. SH1's brief is to encourage the development of your abilities with a view to offering advancement to those of you who, at sixteen, pass your SATs – Super Abilities Tests – whereupon graduates will be given the choice of either becoming trainee super agents or frying onions in a burger bar till they collect their pensions.' He looked down the steps at his wife. 'That bit was a joke,' he said.

'Not one of your finest,' she replied. 'Someone has to fry the onions.'

The Doc looked around at the faces in the courtyard. At a whole lot of stunned expressions.

'Super *agents*?' said one of the students.

'It's not a term that I care for very much,' Withering said, 'but those individuals accepted for employment by SH1 will indeed be something of the sort. They will, I'm told, be issued with an LSP – a Licence to be Super in Public – working to combat crime and terrorism on the country's behalf.'

Another pause, while everyone except Cat (who obviously knew about this already) tried to get their brains round the idea of being super agents working for the government. This pause was ended by Jenny Jones when she asked if SH1 would provide super outfits.

'What do you have in mind?' the Doc asked her.

'Special costumes,' Jenny said. 'Capes and masks and stuff.'

'I don't believe that's been decided yet, but...' He shrugged. 'Who knows?'

'I've said it before and I'll say it again,' said Jamal Sarkis. 'I'm not wearing tights for *anyone*!'

'What if the powers only work when everyone's together?'

The Doc smiled when he heard this, the way he might if this was a room full of four year olds talking about ponies or goblins. But then he realised it was me who'd asked it and the smile turned to dust.

'I don't think I take your meaning, Forty-one.'

'What I *mean*,' I said, 'is do you know for sure that we'll still have powers when we split up?'

'Split up?'

'And leave here. Like, we might have been born with this special gene but until we came here most of us never did anything remotely super, and—'

'Some of us still haven't,' said Saxon Tull, shaking his head sadly at me.

'Tamsin said she changed into a bookend once,' a girl said.

'I did,' said Tamsin, 'and my mum dusted me.'

'I went invisible a couple of times,' said Howley Marsh. 'Think so anyway. A lot of people stopped noticing me.'

'Probably just ignoring you,' someone else said.

'What I'm *saying*,' I went on, more loudly so they had to pay attention, 'is that the powers only started kicking in after we got here. You said it yourself, Doc – '

'Doctor,' he said sternly.

' – it was all of us being here at the same time that made the lights and alarms go wacko.'

'And brought a gargoyle to life,' said Speechless, though no one heard him except me and Cat.

'What if the powers don't work if we aren't near each other?' I continued. 'If we only have powers when there's a bunch of us together. I'm just asking.'

Fair question, I thought, but the Doc looked pretty annoyed by it. Before he could snap an answer, though, his wife said, 'You know, Dax might have something there. If he's right this entire venture could be rendered worthless.'

'Absolutely,' I said. 'So why don't we stop wasting time and order a fleet of taxis and pretend Scragmoor Prime never existed and go back to being normal again?'

'Good try, Forty-one,' said the Doc, 'but until we hear qualified advice to the contrary I think we'll carry on as planned, if it's all the same to you.'

35

'So that's it, and you knew all the time,' I said to Cat when the meeting had clunked to a close. 'We're being groomed as government agents.'

'Oh, I wouldn't call it *groomed*,' she said.

'Call it what you like. I'd rather fry onions.'

Most of the kids had followed the Witherings and the tutors and Miss Piper inside, but a few had trailed off to the moors. The rest – Saxon Tull and three of his disciples, including superfast Rendell Bude, who was standing still for once – still hung about in another part of the courtyard. Byron Flood was one of those who'd gone back indoors, so we decided to take a chance on him tuning in to us all the way out here. He wouldn't have heard much of interest anyway as we were as stuck as ever for what to do about the missing eye. The *false* eye, as we now knew it to be.

'He's standing up,' Speechless said suddenly.

He was staring at the roof. Cat and I looked up too. Saw the gargoyle on his hind legs. We hadn't seen him like that before.

'What's he holding over his head?' Cat wondered.

'Looks like one of those big chunks of stone left by the rioters,' I said.

'Rioters?'

'Old story. I think he's going to chuck it.'

They thought so too. So we walked smartly to the steps, and up them.

'We should warn those boys,' said Speechless.

'Yes,' said Cat. 'Saxon! You others! Get out of the courtyard!'

They looked our way, puzzled, then decided they were being ordered about for the sake of it, and laughed – and stayed where they were.

'Here it comes!' said Speechless, who'd leant out just far enough to see what was happening on the roof.

We were the only ones to hear this, of course, but something made one of the boys look up. He stared for a beat or two, like he was trying to make sense of what he saw, then flung his arms out, struck the two nearest boys in the chest, one per arm, and they – along with him – fell backwards, just out of the line of the plummeting stone. There was just one boy left standing now.

Saxon Tull.

Who gawped at the others rolling on the ground. Like two of them, he had no idea what they were doing there. He also had no idea that in three seconds he would be lying in a bloody heap beneath the stone chunk the gargoyle had hurled. And that's what would have happened if a figure hadn't leapt down the steps, zoomed forward at the speed of something close to light, raised a mighty fist, and smashed the stone to fragments that scattered far and wide.

Tull's jaw dropped as the stone-shattering fist fell to my side. His pals, scrambling to their feet, had seen nothing but the bits of stone flying everywhere. The only person more startled than Tull by what had happened was me. But I couldn't show it. Not to him. I blew on my knuckles, and as I walked away said, for his ears alone, 'Any time you need a hand, Tull – or a fist – you know where to find me.'

Sauntering away quite a bit more casually than I felt, I heard footsteps running after me.

'Dax!' said Speechless as he and Cat caught up.

'That was the most incredible thing ever!'

'The way you ran!' said Cat. 'So fast! And slammed that stone with your fist! And smashed it to bits!'

'Did it hurt?' said Speechless. 'Lemme see, lemme see!'

I showed them my fist. Not a mark on it.

'*Another* power!' Cat said. 'You have four now, counting nearly becoming a gargoyle and the almost flying thing I didn't see. Four, Dax. We're supposed to get one each! One, and you have *four*!'

'They don't last,' I said. 'Not one of them's lasted any time at all.'

'Nobody's has lasted so far. We probably have to learn to use them.'

'Four,' said Speechless. 'And I haven't got one yet.'

'You can speak into people's minds and send feelings and images and pick up messages and stuff,' I reminded him.

'Oh yes, with just two people and a gargoyle. Anyway, that's like Cat's eye deal. I've always had it.'

'I've been thinking about that,' said Cat. 'What if that is my power? What if my Gene kicked in early, and it's all I'm going to get? I mean I might not be in a tearing hurry to *get* a power, but if I don't I'll be letting Dad down.'

'Why, is he counting on it?' I asked.

'It's not that. It's that he got the job running this place because of me having the Gene. It could look like he took it under false pretences.'

'Do the people who gave him the job know about your eyes lighting up and you being able to see in total darkness?'

'I don't think so – why?'

'Well, if it comes to it, you could pretend that's it and you've just got it.'

'Hmmm,' she said. She didn't sound too convinced.

I glanced back at Tull. His buddies were kicking bits of shattered stone about and wondering what just happened. He obviously hadn't told them. He was just standing there, staring after me.

'We're being watched,' said Speechless suddenly.

He didn't mean by Tull. He was squinting up at the roof again. Cat and I looked up too. The gargoyle was back in crouch mode, but his head was raised, like he was following our every move.

'Let's get out of here,' I said.

'We can't go wandering off,' said Cat. 'We've got to find his eye.'

'Yes, and we still don't know where to look for it. Knowing that he was once Spewdrift the hangman and that his eye was false and stolen by a small scowling convict doesn't get us any nearer to knowing where it might be now.'

'Right. We need more time.'

'Which is something he's not gonna give us. So let's talk about it out there, where he can't see us.'

'Out there' was the moor. I hadn't planned it, but we were almost at the gateless gateposts.

'Wait,' said Speechless. 'I'm getting something from the gargoyle.'

'You can hear him from all the way down here?' I asked.

'Seems so.'

'Another of those feelings?'

'No. Words. Actual words. Are you going to fetch my eye?'

'What?'

'That's what he said. What do I tell him?'

'Try the truth. That we're not. That we still haven't

the faintest idea where to look for it.'

'Is that a good idea,' Cat said, 'seeing as we're going out onto the very moor he's promised to put us on for all eternity?'

'I agree,' said Speechless, and closed his eyes.

I asked him what he was doing, but he didn't answer, and a few seconds later we saw the gargoyle sit up straight and flutter his wings.

'What did you tell him?' Cat asked.

'Yes,' said Speechless.

'What do you mean, yes?'

'That we're going to fetch his eye.'

'But we're not.'

'No, but I bought us some time,' he said, and walked swiftly out through the gateless gateposts.

Cat and I walked even more swiftly after him – and past him.

36

The half-dozen kids already on the moor were running and jumping and trying to look like the superheroes they hoped to be when their Gene kicked in. One of the girls even wore a mask and cape. The cape was purple with spangles. If she'd had wings she would have looked like a fairy.

'She'll be so disappointed if she turns into a Hulk,' said Cat.

'Got any powers yet?' one of the kids shouted to us.

'No!' I shouted back.

'Liar,' Cat said.

'No, I mean it. Those things were a fluke. Why would I have four powers while everyone else has one?'

'If they've *even* got one,' grumbled Speechless.

We went to a tor well away from the others. Speechless hauled himself to the top of it while Cat and I sank to the turf and set our backs against a couple of ground-level rocks.

'All right, to business,' Cat said. 'Where would a small convict have hidden the gargoyle's false eye?'

'Spewdrift's false eye,' a voice said in our heads.

'We don't know if it was taken when he was man or gargoyle,' Cat said. 'We *would* have if the person he mentioned it to had bothered to *ask*, but he didn't, so we don't.'

'He might not have remembered which,' I said in my defence.

'No. But he might have. And if he had we'd know whether to look for a gargoyle-size eye or a human-size one. There is a difference, in case you haven't realised.'

'When Spewdrift became a gargoyle,' said Speechless, 'everything about him turned to stone and became whatever size it needed to be – obviously. So the false eye would have too, wouldn't it? But how would anyone get one bit of stone out of another?'

'A chisel?' said Cat.

'A chisel would leave marks round the empty socket. Anyone noticed any marks?'

We hadn't.

'OK,' Speechless said. 'So we're not looking for a

gargoyle-sized eye. But we still don't know what's so special about it. I mean does it *look* special or is it just special to him?'

'Tell you what, why don't we go and ask him?' I said. 'Be a nice change to go up there.'

Suddenly there was a scream off to the right. Then a shout. Then more screams and shouts. The kids over there were running like mad things.

'What's got into them?' Cat said.

'William Brown,' said Speechless from up above.

I stood up. 'Who's William Brown?'

'The one just coming round that tor...'

And round he came – all hunched over and covered in hair, arms hanging low, jaw jutting out, grunting.

I laughed. 'Cat. You have to see this.'

She also got to her feet.

'Turning into an apeman is a super power?' I said. 'Oh boy.'

'Dax,' Cat said quietly.

'What?'

'I hate to tell you this, but...'

'Tell me what?'

She pointed at one of my hands. I looked at it.

Coarse brown hair was growing on it. Fast. I looked at my other hand. Same thing. As I gaped at the hair shooting out of my skin I felt my jaw start to stretch. Then my upper body folded over and my arms swung down to my sides. I tried to speak, but the best I could manage was a grunt.

'Your Lomas Gene really needs to make up its mind,' said Speechless, working his way down from the top of the tor.

He'd only just made it to the ground when the hair shrivelled back into my skin, my long jaw retreated, and I was able stand upright again. I experimented with speech. Words came.

'That just *cannot* be a power. And if it is, I don't want it.'

'People might not notice if it only lasts that long,' said Cat.

'William's still going strong anyway,' said Speechless.

And he was. William Brown was still hairy, still swinging his arms, still loping after the other kids. He turned back into his normal self a minute later, and the others gathered round him, laughing, and flopped down with him on the grass.

'Hey!' said Cat suddenly. 'Look.'

She pointed towards the school. The gargoyle had spread his wings right out and taken off from the roof.

'Looks like he's all powered up now,' I said.

'All powered up and heading this way,' said Speechless, shooting round the back of the tor.

We followed him without a lot of hesitation, and crouched down with him.

'This is your fault,' Cat said to him.

'My fault?'

'You were the one that told him we were coming out here to get his eye.'

'Well how was I to know he could fly?'

'What did you think those wings were for – decoration?'

'They're *stone* wings,' he said.

'Stone or not, they're flapping pretty smoothly now.'

And they were. And carrying the gargoyle over the courtyard and the wall that surrounded the building. A yell off to our right told us that the other kids had also seen him. Then one of the girls – the one dressed like she wanted to be a super fairy – recognised him as the terrifying creature she'd dreamed about that first night, and as the nightmare filled her head all over again she screamed and jumped up, which spooked the others, who also got to their feet. Then they were all running in different directions, panicky directions, and in seconds the only thing to show that they'd been there was the sparkly cape, which had come away in Fairy Girl's terror.

The gargoyle was a lot closer now, but we hoped that if we kept our heads down he would fly right over, across the moor, out of our lives.

He didn't.

He landed some way past our tor, and turned, and saw us, leaving us no choice but to stand up and act casual, like we'd just been taking a little rest.

'Made it off the roof then?' Cat said cheerfully.

'I'm fully alive now,' he said. 'But incomplete. Where is it?'

'Where's what?'

He advanced, slowly, menacingly. 'Do you have it or do you not?' he growled, deep in his throat.

'Oh, your *eye*,' said Cat. 'Well...not quite...not yet. Hot on the trail, though.'

'You think you know where it is?'

Cat looked at me and Speechless. 'Over to you,' she said.

Speechless raised his shoulders to his ears. 'I've got nothing,' he said.

So it was left to me to tell the gargoyle that we'd thought the eye might be out here somewhere, but weren't so sure now, and could we have a little more time, pretty-please.

'Time!' he snarled. 'I've had nothing *but* time on that roof. Time to see but not blink. Time to be subjected to all the elements but feel nothing. And now I have life again. One thing I do *not* have is patience.'

With this he reached for me – just me, because I was the one who'd given him the latest update. The others took a sharp step sideways. Then another.

'Hey, listen,' I said as the gargoyle gripped both of my ankles. 'I'm not the only one failing to find your eye. Feel free to pick on one of them.'

'I don't think heroes are meant to say things

like that,' said Cat.

'OK, so you be a h-h-h-h-hero!' I stammered as
the gargoyle tipped me upside down and shook me
so hard my teeth rattled.

And then he swung me. I think the plan was to
throw me against the tor and do me some serious
damage. Out of the corner of my upside-down eyes

I saw Cat and Speechless spin round and start towards the school at a pace that looked pretty Olympic at a glance.

'Stop!' shouted the gargoyle.

They stopped. Turned round.

'One more step and I'll do to you what I'm now going to do to this one!'

Now here's where I get a chance to use a word I can't often use when talking about myself. That word is 'fortunately'. I can say 'fortunately' because something happened just then that wouldn't have if the gargoyle hadn't been whirling me round his head with the idea of smashing mine against the tor. What happened was that everything in my pockets flew out – a few coins from one, my phone from another, the wooden marbles from the ex-stables from a third.

The gargoyle stopped whirling me, and dropped me.

Thud.

'You *have* found it!' he cried, and pounced on one of the rolling marbles.

'Found it?' Cat said, starting back. 'What do you mean, found it?'

'Oh, you teasers,' the gargoyle said, gazing lovingly at the marble. 'Your idea of a joke, eh? Ho-ho, very funny, highly amusing.'

He plunged the wooden marble into his spare eye socket, but when he took his hand away it popped out again, and dropped to the ground.

'Oh,' he said. 'Of course. It's too small. I didn't think of that.'

He sounded quite disappointed. But he stooped

for the marble anyway, and as he picked it up, his talons began to shrink, and change into...

...fingers.

Human fingers.

And then his bald skull grew hair.

And his wings shrivelled into his back.

And his great muscles shrank.

And his jaw became less pointed.

And then...

He was a man.

A man with the hugest smile you ever saw.

And no clothes.

Not one solitary stitch.

37

'I'm myself again!' the man cried, standing up and looking down at himself.

'Collymore Spewdrift in the flesh,' said Speechless. 'Literally.'

Then the ex-gargoyle looked at the marble in his hand – the blue one with the painted flame – and laughed, and pressed it into his empty eye socket. The marble didn't match his real eye in any way, but he seemed more than happy with it. When he looked at us, with that massive grin and one green eye and one that looked like it had burst into flame, he looked totally insane.

'Is that really what we've been looking for?' Cat asked, staring at the man's face, probably because it was better than staring lower down.

'It is!' he said, and began to dance a jig. 'Oh, well done, thank you, thank you!' He squeezed the marble out again, and looked at it fondly with his green eye. 'If I had two like this I'd be as contented as I'm sure I look.'

'If you had two eyes like that,' I said, 'you wouldn't be able to see.'

'It would be worth it!'

He pressed the marble back into the socket. It went in with a soft *ssshlupp*, like a pebble being forced into wet mud, and somehow, without even checking to make sure it was right, he made the painted flame face out once more.

Cat glared. At me. 'You had it all the time. All that wondering, all the chat, the visits to the roof, the trouble we've taken, and you had it *all the time!*'

'Ouch! Speechless knew about it too,' I said, rubbing the shoulder she'd punched.

'You nicked it,' he said. 'It was in your pocket.'

Cat stalked to the sparkly cape dropped by the girl who wanted to be a super fairy. 'Wrap this round you,' she said, tossing it to Mr Spewdrift. 'And I don't mean your shoulders.'

He tied it round his waist in a neat bow. A little purple cape covered in spangles might not have been the top fashion pick of an ex-gargoyle, but it was a definite improvement on nothing at all.

'So how come you're human again?' I asked,

scooping up my phone and coins but leaving the last two marbles.

'I neither know nor care,' he said, smiling fit to split his face in two. 'It is sufficient that I am.'

'Maybe it was getting his eye back,' Speechless suggested.

'A piece of painted wood?' I said.

'My money's on the accumulated Lomas Genes,' said Cat. 'Their combined power. First they soften the stone, then activate his brain and voice box, then give him the power of flight, and finally...the apparition we see before us.'

'Whatever did it, we're OK now, right?' Speechless said to Mr Spewdrift. 'You won't be turning us to stone and leaving us out here for all eternity?'

Spewdrift laughed. Not the harsh, deep, dark laugh of a mean gargoyle but the jolly, musical laugh of a man who's seriously delighted with the way things have turned out.

'Turn you to stone?' he said. 'How could I, now that I'm human again? And to tell you the truth, I couldn't have done it as a gargoyle either.'

'What?'

He laughed again. 'The best I could manage then was to chuck the odd bit of stone off the roof and look cranky.'

'And the threat to pile everyone on top of each other to make tors...?'

He almost chortled his head off at that. 'That was a good one, wasn't it?'

Cat frowned. 'So we needn't have bothered looking for your eye at all.'

Spewdrift wrinkled his nose at her. 'Awfully good of you to do that for little me.'

'Have you got all your memory back now?' I asked.

'Indeed I have! Collymoor Spewdrift, hangman of Scragmoor, is complete in mind and body once again!'

'*Life-taker* of Scragmoor,' said Cat sourly.

'Those prisoners' names you gave us,' I said, and turned to Speechless for them.

'Gawkson, Bone, Morgan, Little Jamie,' he said.

'Yes. Were they all hanged by you?'

Spewdrift looked startled for a sec, then said: 'Gawkson, Bone and Morgan were condemned men delivered to me, but Little Jamie? He *certainly* wasn't a prisoner!'

I was about to ask who Little Jamie was if he wasn't a prisoner, when Speechless got in first with a question about someone else. When he heard this name Spewdrift came over all thoughtful, and as sad-looking as anyone can with a smile as huge and crazy as his.

'Dear Sally Anne,' he said. 'Dear, dear, *dear* Sally Anne.'

'Who's Sally Anne?' Cat asked Speechless.

'His wife.'

She turned back to Spewdrift. 'Why have a false eye that doesn't look like an eye, and what happened to the one it replaced? The real one.'

'Would you like me to tell you?' he said.

'After all you've put us through I think that's the least you could do.'

'Then I shall. Be seated, best beloved, and harken to the tale of Collymore Jeremiah Spewdrift!'

For many years I was a sailor, and in my time I sailed five of the seven seas on a dozen ships of various size and quality. I was an amiable chap in general, but never with those who mocked my sunny visage by calling me Smiler. One night, in the port of Cadiz, I was drawn into conflict with a ruffian who made light of the warm turn of my lips, and during our disagreement he got the advantage of me and dug out one of my eyes with his blade. For a long time I wore a patch over the vacancy, but then, in 1892, in the South Pacific, I jumped ship and while strolling the black sands of Tahiti, met a Frenchie who was a painter and woodcarver, and we fell to talking and drinking together, and in return for my allowing him to paint me, he fashioned a wonderful eyeball for me, and painted it blue with a bright flame to warm my days in colder climes, and here it is (tap, tap).

I sailed on other vessels and oceans after that, proudly sporting my perfect eye, until a ship I served upon docked at a port not many miles from this moor, and there I met Sally Anne, the first woman to admire both my constant smile and my beautiful eye. We set up home together in a small cottage on the moor and I obtained work as a carpenter and rope maker, and in time, when Bittern the Younger lost his position, I took his place as hangman at the Jail – employment which, though part-time, I proved well suited to. I was very conscientious in my work for Governor Hext, taking pains to ensure that my trapdoor never stuck and my ropes were sound and well knotted. No man, woman or child hanged by me suffered more than half a minute, and more often than not their end was instantaneous, which I'm sure you'll agree is testament to my skill.

But as my working life on dry land became more agreeable, my domestic situation deteriorated. Sally Anne, such a sweetie when we met, began to complain of having no distraction from a dull life, and never seeing another living soul apart from a neighbouring family she did not get on with, and before long her tongue was lashing me mercilessly whenever I was home, ranting about the smallest thing – a speck of mud on a boot sole, the fray of a cuff, an item of clothing not hung up or put away – until a day came when she informed me that she could no longer bear to see my perfect eye and unwavering smile. This, the final humiliation, led to my setting fire to the neighbouring cottage and planting evidence of my darling as the culprit. Of course the firing of a building might not have released me entirely from her vicious slurs and critical glare, but fortunately the whole family – all four of them – was home that night, so Sally Anne was convicted at the Assizes not only of arson, but of multiple homicide.

When the day dawned on which my dear was brought before me in the Shed, I encircled her neck with a rope of finest quality, which I'd paid for personally and adorned with a pink ribbon just for her. She did not thank me, however, but cursed the day she ever saw my cheerful smile and glorious eye, which cut me deeply. Yet, to show there were no hard feelings, I gave her a little longer than most to kick upon the rope, and even went down below the trap before the end to send her on her way with one last loving smile. Then, when she was neatly tucked into the wooden box I'd fashioned for her with my own hands, I returned to our silent cottage and put my muddy feet upon Sally Anne's freshly ironed tablecloth, in homage to her.

Now you'll be wondering how I lost my eye. Well, as you're sitting so attentively, I'll tell you.

I had no children of my own and became very attached to the governor's three, and they to me. Mr Hext – a generous man with an infectious chuckle – was happy for me to show them games and tricks and dances picked up on my travels in the world. I spent a deal of time with Daisy, Miranda and young James – particularly after Sally Anne's departure from this world – and we had a fine time playing Battledore & Shuttlecock, Charades, Tiddlywinks and Tug-o'-War (the three of them against me, ha-ha!). I would also make them squeal sometimes by popping out my Tahitian eye and dancing with it on the tips of my fingers. They were fascinated by my eye, especially James. He admired the flame painted by my artist friend so much that he made little pictures of his own on some of his wooden marbles, which, as it happened, were almost identical in size and shape to my eye. I think I saw a couple of them on the ground back there, but I can't be sure.

A favourite game of the children was Hide-and-Seek, with me the quarry more often than not. One afternoon I climbed up to the roof and crouched alongside the old gargoyle that leaned out over the edge. The children were sharp, though, and they tracked me all the way, but I might yet have fooled them had not a storm brewed too rapidly, as storms do on Scrag Moor. The children were on the roof too, but they hadn't seen me and were about to give up when a sharp flash of lightning made me jump – I was ever the nervy one – and fall against the gargoyle, and as I fell my flaming eye popped out. The children saw this, and James, little Jamie, rushed forward and snatched it – just for a laugh, you understand – and he and the girls skipped down the ladder in triumph. They were barely out of sight, however, when my shape began to change to one similar to that of the grotesque I'd fallen against, and my flesh to harden, while he, the gargoyle, took the form of a man, who stood up, and threw his arms in the air, and cried, 'At last!'

The man who'd been a gargoyle was not bothered by his nakedness, or by the lightning, or the thunder. So pleased was he to resume the shape that had once been his that he told me, with some relish, of his parents, the brothers he'd had, and how, as my own history began

274

to fade from my mind, it was he who designed the building whose roof I now crouched upon in his stead. He was about to go on his way, descend the ladder and go out into the world once more, when he came over faint and said that he felt unwell, and sat down beside me on the edge of the roof. Sitting there, he grew less and less talkative, and finally, in a very frail voice, said, 'Oh, but of course, I'm old now, so very old...'

Now my neck was not yet as rigid as it would become, and I saw his eyes grow dim, and his skin shrivel like paper burned with cold fire. And then the flesh beneath the dry skin opened up, and soon, as all the living matter peeled or dripped from the bones within, there was nothing left of him but his skeleton, brown with the age it would have been had it lain in a grave for a century and a half, or more. And then he toppled backwards, off the roof, and I leaned out and saw his skeleton shatter in the courtyard below, his disconnected skull roll away, bump-bump-bump, across the cobbles. As I watched I felt my own flesh harden utterly, compelling me to remain in that position – leaning out, staring sightlessly – for what felt like...

What year is this?

39

When Spewdrift had finished his tale, Cat asked what he planned to do now.

'In truth, I'm not sure,' he answered. 'I might return to sea again, and travel. I imagine the world's changed a little since my day.'

'What'll you do for money and clothes?' Speechless asked.

'Oh, I was ever a resourceful chap, I'm sure I'll get by.'

'You're much nicer in that body than when you were a gargoyle,' Cat said.

'But of course. Gargoyles and nice don't mix. One has one's image to protect, after all. And I have to admit, I...'

He stopped, drew a sharp breath, and went very pale.

'What's up?' Cat asked.

Spewdrift leant back against the tor we were sitting around. 'It must be all the excitement. The switch from stone to flesh after such a time. I'll rest a while before I...before I depart.'

'All right, well, if there's nothing we can do...'

'No, no, you've been...you've been very kind.'

'Look after that eye,' said Speechless. 'Hate you to lose it a second time.'

Spewdrift gave a wheezy little laugh. 'Me too.'

We got up, and as we walked away I said, 'I can't believe you two are even giving him the time of day. How do we know that when he's away from here he won't do other stuff, as bad as the things he just told us?'

'What do you suggest?' said Cat. 'Tell the cops he killed people in the 19th century, then took a job as a rooftop gargoyle for a hundred and something years, but he's back now? No, all we can do is make sure he's well away from here and out of our hair.'

'And in someone else's?'

She shrugged. 'Their problem.'

'Hey, Dax,' said Speechless. 'The skull in the ex-stables. Care to bet it isn't the architect's?'

'There's a skull in the ex-stables?' Cat asked.

'In the display cabinet,' I said.

'Ooh, how gross.'

'And the underground exhibition and the Hanging Shed aren't?'

'Yeah, but a *skull*? On *display*?'

'Here's a thought,' said Speechless. 'According to Spewdrift, when the first gargoyle turned back into the architect, his flesh rotted away in no time and what was left of him took a speedy dive off the roof. Why do you think he became a skeleton so soon after getting his human form back?'

'Well, because he was so far past his natural lifetime's sell-by date,' I said. 'What else could it be?'

'Exactly. And Spewdrift, born when *he* was, would be pretty bony himself by now if he hadn't been a gargoyle all these years.'

Cat and I skidded to a halt. Speechless stopped too.

'He did look a bit off-colour when we left him,' said Cat.

'Didn't sound all that hearty either,' I said.

We spun around and started back. Approaching the tor, we saw no sign of Collymore Spewdrift.

'The sparkly little cape's still there,' Cat pointed out.

'Maybe he felt better after we left and decided to

explore the world in the nuddy,' I said.

'If he did, he'll probably get locked up anyway.'

But that wasn't it, and we sort of knew it already. Back at the tor we found, lying on its side, partly covered by the sparkly cape, an old brown skeleton.

We stood around for a minute saying things like 'Whew' and 'Wow'. Then Cat said: 'What do we do

with it? I mean, do we say a few words, give it a decent burial, stuff like that?'

'He doesn't deserve any of that,' I said. 'Think of all the people he killed.'

'It was his job,' said Speechless.

'I don't mean as a hangman, though that's bad enough.'

'True. Let's leave him to rot.'

'I think he already has.'

'People will wonder what an old skeleton's doing here,' said Cat.

'Well, we know nothing about it, do we?' I said.

We were about to leave when I noticed something small and round, blue and red, that had rolled out of the skull and away a bit. I stooped to pick it up – but hesitated. Did I really want to handle an eyeball, even a false one, that had been in a living socket so recently?

But then I thought, 'It's art,' and grabbed it.

Put it back in my pocket.

4

It's evening, and I'm up on the roof, sitting cross-legged where the gargoyle once crouched. I've been at Scragmoor Prime for three weeks, and almost half the students have got powers now. Some of the powers are amazing, some are kind of wacky, and four or five are just insane, like Robbie Strogatz's. (Robbie turns to water every time the sun comes out, so he stays indoors on sunny days.) The first kids to get powers are learning to use them and activate them when they want, which doesn't lift the hearts of those who haven't got any yet, like Cat, who's getting a teensy bit grumpy about not having what she calls a 'proper power'. Speechless is a bit better off than her. He can speak into six kids' minds now. The rest, the ones who haven't got a power yet, are looking forward to the day they get theirs. No one knows who's going to get what power, or when. The only thing that's clear is that it's just one power each. One power for everyone. Everyone except...

Dax Daley.

That should make me pretty special, you'd think.

Oh yes? Really?

No. *Not* really.

Because I've had time to realise something about my Lomas Gene. It isn't running through the powers one by one trying to find the one that's right for me. It's not doing that because I'm the only Scragmoor student who isn't going to *get* a power.

Uh?

Yes.

Every power that's come to me has been someone else's. I borrow powers from those who have them. I don't want to, I don't try to, I just do. Like when Marcus Preedy took off from the courtyard that day I left the ground too, but when he wasn't around the best I could do was lift my heels. And when I got super speed it came from Rendell Bude. And when I smashed the chunk of stone with my fist, Saxon Tull was there. And when I went ape for half a minute...

Well, you get the idea. I soak up other people's powers. The Human Sponge, that's me. How's that for a hero name? I don't know whose power I'm going to borrow next, or when. The only people apart from

Cat and Speechless who've seen me with any power are Marcus – who seems to have forgotten – and Tull, who keeps it to himself. Tull probably doesn't want it getting about that I might have strength to match his.

Still, even if I don't have a power of my own, I don't hate being here any more. Not as much anyway. Things are turning out to be just a bit more interesting than they were back home. So maybe I'll stick around for a while. There is one thing I wonder about, though, sitting up here on the roof. What if the power that almost turned me into a gargoyle is still tucked away inside me? If it is, how do I know I won't become a fully-formed gargoyle between winks of a non-gargoyle eye?

Imagine that. Dax Daley, Scragmoor Gargoyle Number Three!

I think I hear a chuckle at my elbow as that thought occurs. But I chuckle too, and take Spewdrift's eyeball out of my pocket. The blue one with the painted flame. I hold it up, and in the fading evening light it seems to flare for a second, just for me, like it's sharing a joke, or a secret. I lean forward, almost to the edge of the roof, and draw a number in the dust with the eye of the gargoyle. The number of someone who wasn't meant to be here.

41

I've got used to that. It's who I am now. But even I don't know quite what Hero 41 is capable of.

Yet.

Don't miss Dax's next adventure at
SCRAGMOOR PRIME!

Coming soon!

Read on for a sneak peek…

If ever a place was just perfect for bad dreams it was Scragmoor. And the dream I had that night was a doozy. And so vivid. Like I was living every second of it, from the moment I started to roll off my mattress, realised just in time that I wasn't on the floor, and climbed down the little ladder instead.

It wasn't that I needed to go anywhere, it was just something I found myself doing. Had to do. I put my slippers on, my dressing gown, opened the door, went out. I didn't turn right and go to the bathroom, like I usually do if I wake in the night, but left, past the rest of the bedcells, and down the stairs to the lobby – quietly, so I wouldn't wake anyone. I went from there to the Infirmary. Then to the door to the dungeons. I opened the door, turned the light on, went down the old stone stairs. There was no one else down there, just me and rows of cells with waxwork prisoners in them, lying down or sitting up or standing around looking suicidal. At any other time I would have been pretty spooked down there alone at night, but I felt nothing as I walked past the cells, round the corner, past more cells, to the door at the end.

The door to the underground tunnel.

It was closed, of course, but I reached for the handle, and as I reached I started to experience a kind of worry, and hesitated, and as I hesitated I heard a sound some way behind me. I didn't turn, though. I didn't look back. I couldn't somehow. All I knew was that I had to go into the tunnel. I turned the handle. Pushed the door back. There was no light the other side. Nothing at all but total, endless blackness. But there was something. Something tall. Waiting for me.

I took a forward step.

But just one step. Then froze.

I froze because suddenly I could hear boots scraping the stone floor ahead of me, and gruff voices cursing, and a laugh from one of them, and then... there were men carrying boards with bodies on them, dead bodies, corpses, along the black tunnel, towards the room at the end.

All this filled my head as I stood with one foot inside the doorway, and as I stood there, listening to the men and watching them carry the bodies away, it came to me that I was about to go the same way as the dead, to the room, and up the stairs to the chapel, then outside, to an oblong Dax-sized hole with a small stone at the head of it. A stone with my name on it.

It was about then that I realised something else.

That I wasn't dreaming...